Sparks and Ashes

Short Fiction

Alby Stone

Swansong (25 November 2012), *Time Travel for Beginners* (8 December 2012), *The Ray* (7 November 2012), *Companions* (15 November 2012), *The Devil's Verse* (7 November 2013), *L'Histoire Perdue* (14 February 2014), *Shots* (15 February 2013), *Milestone* (6 June 2013), *Copy Error #47* (26 November 2013), *Et in Arcadia Ego* (9 March 2013), *The Tiger's Birthday* (1 May 2013), *Ringbanen* (28 August 2013), *Post-It* (22 October 2012), *In the Beginning was the Word* (20 January 2013), and *Touching the Zero* (22 December 2012) were all previously published on the Vainglorious Lunacy website.
http://vaingloriouslunacy.com

Asking (29 January 2013) was previously published on the Clerkenwell Writers Asylum website.

http://clerkenwellwritersasylum.wordpress.com/

Pants, *Walkin' Back to Happiness*, *The Other Side of the River* and *Mighty Boy* are published here for the first time.

Copyright © 2012, 2013, 2014 Alby Stone

All rights reserved.

ISBN-10: 1499201974
ISBN-13: 978-1499201970

Contents

Introduction i
Swansong 1
Time Travel For Beginners 12
The Ray 20
Companions 25
The Devil's Verse 34
L'Histoire Perdue 51
Asking 65
Shots 71
Milestone 86
Copy Error #47 91
Et In Arcadia Ego 105
Pants 118
The Tiger's Birthday 125
Walkin' Back to Happiness 135
Ringbanen 142
The Other Side of the River 157
Post-It 164
In the Beginning was the Word 177
Touching the Zero 184
Mighty Boy 194

Introduction

OK, let's keep this short.

The stories in this book were written, revised and generally bullied or beaten into their present shape between May 2011 and April 2014. Most have previously appeared on the Vainglorious Lunacy or Clerkenwell Writers Asylum websites. A few have been corrected or lightly revised for this collection. Four stories are published here for the first time.

I'd like to say a special thank-you to Shirley Phillips for correcting my French for *L'Histoire Perdue*.

Alby Stone
Walworth, London
April 2014

Swansong

My name is Ivan Grigorovich Lebedye. I was born in Moscow in 1970, the son of a policeman and a hairdresser. I applied myself at school and at university and did well. Until recently I was a history teacher at a prestigious school in Ekaterinburg. I had a beautiful wife, Mariya; and two young children, girls who I was sure would grow up to be as lovely and clever as their mother. They used to sing all the time and so I called them my three little songbirds. In my spare time I wrote books – a few historical studies, a couple of modestly successful genre novels under another name – and occasionally taught Russian history to American and British students for a few extra dollars. I became reasonably wealthy, earning more than enough money for my family to live well, and our prospects seemed excellent. I was happy and contented, with so much to look forward to.

One summer day in 2008, Chechen terrorists detonated an explosive device on a train between Ekaterinburg and Moscow. Dozens of people were killed, many more horribly injured and maimed. My wife had been taking our girls, only four and six years old, to visit their grandparents in Moscow while I was at home writing my latest history book. The blast destroyed my family in an instant and the best part of my life was taken away with them. I remember little of the weeks that followed. I drank a lot of vodka – a lot of vodka – but it would not deaden my blossoming pain nor could it fill the emptiness in my soul.

After a few months I decided that my family would not have wanted me to descend to being a mindless drunk pissing himself in the gutter. God knows Russia has always had enough of those. I wanted the shades of my wife and daughters to be proud of me. I did not want to shame their memory by abandoning my life and giving in forever to despair and misery. I pulled myself together, though it was not easy, and regained a measure of control over my emotions. I went back to work. Indeed, I immersed myself in work – teaching at the school, staying up until the early hours researching and writing. To ease the loneliness I took on more students.

At the school my colleagues and students were polite but tended to give me a wide berth – I think many people have an unspoken belief that grief is infectious – and I was left to get on with my work. There were a few dutiful social invitations, but everyone seemed almost relieved when I declined them and eventually they ceased altogether. I must have seemed a strange figure to my American and British private clients, distant and distracted, somehow not entirely present. They adapted, I carried on.

A few months into my resumed life I happened to mention to one of my private students that I was thinking of doing some work on the contrasts and parallels between British and Russian social history of the late nineteenth century. In particular, I wanted to focus on ordinary middle-class families – most social histories of the time focused on either the plight of the working poor or the wealthy capitalists and innovators, while the history of the aristocracy, their wars, insanities and vanities, had been mined to exhaustion. I wanted to take two families that represented the hard-working, under-represented middle class of both countries and see how they compared.

To my surprise, one of my students – a young woman whose name I shall omit – told me that she had been engaged in researching her ancestors and had plenty of documented information that she would be happy to turn over to me. Over dinner at one of the better restaurants in Ekaterinburg, she told me more about her family. I was intrigued to learn that the daughter of one of her great-great-grandmothers' sisters had been married to a schoolteacher in England in the late nineteenth century. This sounded ideal – a subject to which I could relate both personally and professionally. I asked if she had any documents relating to the family at that time. She promised to e-mail me what she had. The evening ended cordially – and chastely, in case you are wondering – and I made my way home full in the belly and more optimistic than I had been for a long time.

The next day I received an e-mail with several attachments – scanned copies of registry entries, birth, marriage and death certificates, and newspaper reports; and a lengthy Word document. I read through the document with growing interest, and a faint stirring of unease.

One section of the text told the story of how my

student's great-great-grandmother's younger sister Mary Victoria Smith had married thirty-one year-old John Swan, known as 'Jack', a teacher by profession according the marriage certificate, in 1872. In the space of three years after the marriage Mary had borne two girls. In 1879, Mary and her daughters, then aged four and six, died in a train crash just outside London. Jack Swan also came to an untimely end: in 1889 he was found dead in an alley off the Strand. Doctors were unable to establish a cause of death.

The similarities to my own situation were apparent. The unfortunate Mr Swan had married at the same age I had, fathered two girls who were born two years apart, and lost his wife and children to a fatal incident involving a train when his daughters were the same ages mine had been. The coincidence was remarkable enough, but when one considers that my first name is the Russian equivalent of John, and that my family name, Lebedye, is the Russian word for 'swan', it seemed more than happenstance.

This was clearly a sick joke. I was distressed and enraged.

The next time I saw the woman who had given me those materials, I asked if she knew anything about my personal history. She replied that she knew I was recently bereaved but claimed ignorance of any details. She also reiterated that the documentary evidence was genuine. I was still suspicious, however, and told her that I was unable to use her material and advised her that I would be unable to tutor her any further. She was upset but I could not continue to teach someone I thought might be having a good laugh at my expense. I abandoned my history project, which had now acquired unpleasant associations, and tried once more to get on with my life, such as it was.

A year or so later, having put that sour episode behind me, I decided that I would like to travel. I had flown to New York as an exchange student many years before but apart from a brief trip to Poland and another to Budapest, I hadn't seen much of the world outside the old Soviet Union countries. I had money and no one to leave it to, so I thought I might as well make good use of it. And make use of it I did – I flew to Istanbul, hired a car and drove through Turkey, going from one historic site to another: Gallipoli, Hissarlik, Afrodisias, Ephesos, Pamukkale, Cappadocia and Göbekli Tepe. It was wonderful. For a few weeks I almost forgot my ever-smouldering grief and considered perhaps retraining as an archaeologist. I became enamoured of the landscape, the strange amalgam of modernity, Islam and medieval tribalism, and developed a taste for the local food and cigarettes. I thought I might even grow a moustache, which seemed always to be fashionable among Turkish men.

Eventually I found myself back in Istanbul. The morning before I was due to return to Russia was very hot and I fancied a beer. A short distance from my hotel I found a little bar. Above the main window was a picture of a swan, which made me smile. It seemed like a good omen.

The man serving at the bar was tall and brawny but with a melancholy expression. He looked about sixty years old and his moustache was nearer white than grey. He spoke to me in Turkish. I replied in English that I didn't speak his language. He gave me a doleful look and asked, in good but strongly-accented English, what I wanted. I ordered an Efes beer.

'You have a Russian accent,' he said. 'I have many Russian customers – many businessmen, some street girls. I speak a little Russian, but only a little. My English is much better.'

I paid for my beer and gave a generous tip. I told him that I had come into his bar because my name was the Russian word for a swan. His sad face softened slightly and he looked almost amused. He told me that his name was Mehmet Kuğu – the swan sign was, he said, because his own family name meant 'swan'. I laughed, delighted at this coincidence. 'Don't tell me you have a brother named Ivan,' I joked.

'My brother Yunus is dead for many years, since I was a young man myself,' Mehmet lowered his eyes and shook his head sadly. 'He was found dead in his bed one morning. We never found out what killed him. His eyes were open and there wasn't a mark on him. It was as if he'd just come to a stop. Only forty-eight years old. It was a blessing that his wife and daughters could not be there to see it.'

An alarm bell tolled in my head. It was silent yet it drowned out my thoughts. I stopped drinking. I couldn't breathe. For one moment I think even my heart stopped beating and the blood was becalmed in my veins. The sunlit bar suddenly seemed unaccountably dark.

'I'm so sorry,' I said when I had regained something of my composure. 'That must have been a terrible thing for you. What happened to his wife and children?'

Mehmet shook his head again. 'Poor Meral and her little girls were killed when Kurdish terrorists blew up a train. They were just four and six years old. Yunus was destroyed. He used to call them his three little birds, always singing. We made it a joke. Swans shouldn't be able to sing like angels.' He added that Yunus and Meral had married when Yunus was thirty-one and that Meral had given birth to the first child around eleven months after the wedding. 'Only a few years he had them, then he too was gone.'

Slowly and with another beer to settle me, I told him my own story. I showed him the photograph I always carry in my wallet. Then I told him about John Swan who died in London. He turned away and poured a glass of whisky, which he drained in one swift gulp. Fumbling inside his shirt he drew out an amulet, a circular blue object with what looked like eyes around the rim. He pointed at me.

'This is not a good thing. I think you had better go now and not come back.' There was a note of finality in his voice. His hands were trembling.

Two such similar stories might be accepted as coincidence, even three. But there is a point where coincidence simply cannot be invoked to explain away the facts. Since that day in Istanbul I have made further disturbing discoveries. I have many contacts abroad – as a Russian scholar I learned long ago that reliable information was best located outside my country's borders – and have made extensive use of the internet. I have learned of Jean Cygné, who was found dead in his bath in 1979. Cygné's wife and daughters had been killed in a train crash ten years earlier. Sean Swann of Limerick collapsed and died in the street in 1840, ten years after his wife and young girls had died in a coaching accident. Then I learned of Johann Schwan of Bremen, Juan Cisne of Alicante, Ion Lebeda of Timișoara...

There are many more: some are consecutive, with one 'John Swan' born the year after a previous one has died, in what seems to be an endless cycle; some overlap in time. At first I tried to trace all the lineages, so to speak, but found them baffling, with many gaps that might only be filled by trawling through records in every town and village on the face of the planet, which would be an impossible task. All these men were teachers. All were married at thirty-one, fathers at thirty-two, bereaved at thirty-eight through accidents or assaults involving transport that killed their wives and their daughters of four and six years. All died mysteriously at forty-eight. Wherever I have been able to determine more than the bare details, the girls and their mother were noted for their singing. I have found many other John Swans, of course, but this curse only seems to affect those who are teachers and marry at the age of thirty-one.

What is happening? Does some unfathomable law of mathematics or physics kick in so that when teachers named John Swan decide to marry at the age of thirty-one they are doomed to lose their wives and daughters when – like swans – they are migrating? Or is some other force at work? Who or what decides that everything in their lives from that moment on has to conform to this bizarre cycle? Is some vast and unknowable intelligence punishing swans who teach? Does some unimaginable creature somewhere out there in the depths of space and time hate swans that sing?

In the course of my researches I have discovered that swans were associated with death and the underworld in many ancient cultures, and that the constellation Cygnus was once widely thought to be the entrance to the land of the dead. That is ominous enough. But then you have the swansong, the cries folklore says swans make when they are about to die. Furthermore, swans don't really sing – they make a cacophonous racket that can sometimes sound relatively harmonious but you couldn't really call it singing. I suppose you have to be another swan to appreciate it.

Folktales from Ireland to Japan tell of women who are transformed into swans. The shamans of Siberia tell how the spirits of the dead can take the shape of swans. I do not believe in these tales, though it would comfort me to know that my wife and daughters have grown snow-white wings and remain happy and beautiful as they soar through the air. It would be nice to think that one day, when my time comes, I might sprout feathers myself and rejoin them.

I'm an atheist, a materialist. I was very nearly a good Marxist-Leninist, until *perestroika* came along to teach me the unexpected error of my ways. I don't believe in gods or supernatural agencies. I don't believe that supernatural agencies or cosmic intelligences guide our thoughts and direct our hands. I do believe that science and mathematics can help us understand both the universe and ourselves. But what I have found in my researches confounds me. I am lost in it, marooned in a terrifying sea of doubt and dreadful wonder. The facts are there, solid and undeniable. And they point to one thing: that my death is already scripted.

I have written to everyone named John Swan or the local equivalent that I have been able to locate, in almost every country in the world, warning them to avoid becoming teachers or at least to avoid marrying at thirty-one at all costs. Hopefully that will save lives and avoid much grief and heartbreak. I myself have less than a month to live unless I can find a way out. Some of the coach and train crashes in which the women and children died appeared accidental but many others were not, the work of terrorists or bandits. If some were suspicious, then surely all must be. Logically, that means that none of my namesakes' deaths can be treated as natural. There are many ways to make cold-blooded murder look like a heart attack or a stroke, and not all are modern inventions. I am forced by a chain of reason to conclude that my death will not be an act of God, but of a Devil. Yet that chain is as flimsy as a cobweb.

The day before my forty-eighth birthday I moved to a small *dacha* I had built far out in a remote part of the Siberian *taiga*, far from any towns, a long way away from such roads as there are in the Siberian forest. It took the last of my money and a substantial loan, but the *dacha* is well-appointed and quite well fortified. Around it I have set trip-wires and other devices that will alert me to any intruders. Here, in isolation and far from any other human beings, I wait with loaded guns. I shall re-emerge only when I reach my forty-ninth birthday. That will be twenty-seven days from today.

I do not know who or what might come for me. I do not know how many there will be. If human, they will be dealt with and disposed of. Those who killed my wife and children will deserve it. The vast and largely unpopulated *taiga* is a good place to bury bodies. But although I am sure my namesakes' families died at the hands of human beings,

I do not know what guided those hands and to what lengths it would be prepared to go to ensure that my death conforms to the pattern it has set.

Something very strange is happening here. It is only July but in the last few days I have seen large numbers of Tundra Swans in the vicinity. It is far too early in the year for them to migrate. They are far from their normal habitat and there are no rivers or lakes nearby, only small streams and pools. At night I hear them nearby, the soft bark of the Bewick's Swan and the high-pitched honk of the other sub-species, the Whistling Swan. I glimpse them flitting through the birch trees and ferns like ghosts. Their feathers appear magically around the *dacha* like unseasonal snow. Sometimes their calls merge and become almost musical. Now and then they seem to form words, and their sounds become almost like voices. Among them are voices I know well. They are calling me.

Time Travel for Beginners

'So how did it go?' The young assistant was curious.

'It went OK,' the Director spoke through a mouthful of pizza. 'We hit the target location and time almost exactly. The new programming ensured we had a preview of the area before materialising, so we could choose our position. Now we know that works, there won't be any repeat of the Dallas incident.'

The Director was referring to an earlier trial during which the Ackroyd Mechanics Time Machine transport cage had materialised in the Texas School Book Depository one afternoon in the November of 1963. A startled Lee Harvey Oswald had stared open-mouthed at the shimmering cage and the travellers silhouetted against the light pulsing from the drive, and fled in terror leaving his rifle lying on the floor by the open window. One of the team had been required to return to the same time and had finished the job with a couple of bullets fired from the Grassy Knoll. The ethical dilemma had been debated with heat and intensity but in the end the team had agreed, reluctantly but unanimously, that history had to be served. If John F. Kennedy was assassinated that day, then someone had to have shot him. A reconnaissance trip had found the Grassy Knoll to be empty of other lone gunmen, so there was nothing else for it. The Director himself had fired the historic bullets. He'd felt oddly proud of himself when he pulled the trigger.

The assistant was an ambitious but diplomatic young woman and keen to keep on the good side of her boss, so she didn't mention the Sarajevo fiasco – there had been no plot to kill the Archduke until time travellers from 2016 had discovered that there was no plot in 1914 – or the Rendlesham Forest affair, when a malfunctioning transport cage had sparked a major security incident near a USAAF base in East Anglia that was still widely interpreted as a UFO crash.

There had been other such incidents. In their private moments, both the Director and his assistant wondered how much of the world's history had actually been caused by members of their team – past, present and future – ironing out what they perceived to be wrinkles in the smooth, familiar fabric of the known past. According to the principles of the Grandfather Paradox, they would never know, as they were now living in a timeline in which those events occurred. According to the latest version of the 'many worlds' theory, there were whole universes where JFK lived to a ripe old age; where the First World War had never happened and consequently there had been no Third Reich, no Russian Revolution, and no state of Israel – perhaps it was a largely peaceful world. Or perhaps it was a world where the old imperialist powers vied with America for global supremacy, most of their citizens locked in serfdom and slavery. They would never know. At least that's what the Director said. His assistant didn't really understand what it all meant.

The Director chewed the last mouthful of pizza and threw the box into a waste bin. A stray sliver of onion fell to the floor, ignored. The assistant glared at him – the man might be brilliant but he was a slob. He was also arrogant and selfish. She briefly fantasised about using the transport cage to visit the infant Director and administer a few chastening and potentially life-changing slaps, maybe even give the man's mother a piece of her mind. As she dreamed of pre-emptive character building, the Director fiddled with a computer keyboard, snapped a few peremptory orders that she didn't hear, then left the control room. It was exactly one o'clock in the afternoon – time for the Director's daily lunchtime meeting with the Chairman's secretary in one of the storage rooms.

His assistant waited until he had closed the door behind him then sat down at the control panel. She was not only ambitious – she was vindictive and vengeful, and had a huge grudge against her grandfather. When she was only a little girl Grandad had begun to creep into her bedroom in the middle of the night. The abuse began when she was eight and continued until she was twelve – after her first menstruation the old bastard had lost interest in her. She wasn't allowed to tell her mum, he had told her, because then she would get into trouble. Not that her mum would have been much use – she was a timid, fragile woman whose main interests in life had always been escapist television and Valium. No wonder her father hadn't hung around, whoever he was. So she had endured the pain, the fear and the humiliation, and had suffered in silence throughout her life, mistrustful and afraid to form relationships. An outwardly good-natured woman, if prone to sullenness, inside she had grown into a seething bundle of anger and resentment. And for that she could not be blamed.

She hated her grandfather and wished he had died long before she was born. Sitting at that control panel day after day, she had begun to form an idea. Ackroyd Mechanics had changed the world with this device, she mused. History was now as exact a science as engineering and mathematics, and there had been talk of the police using it to solve crimes, though that was controversial and would have to be tightly regulated. Access to the past was strictly regulated and interference of any kind was wholly forbidden, except to correct mistakes. Still, it would be nice to go back and erase the horrible old bastard before he even had the faintest sniff of starting on her. Who would ever know?

She opened the software that ran the AcMe TM and considered her options. The best thing would be to make it look like an accident – maybe an overzealous mugging as he walked home from that shop he had managed years ago, a long way from her in space and time. Or maybe she could push him down the stairs one night, waiting for him on the landing, in the dark. Undetectable – the perfect crime and some righteous vengeance. His death surely wouldn't affect history – he had been an idle, useless waste of space whose only talents lay in shouting drunkenly at terrified shop assistants and acting out his sexual fantasies on a defenceless little girl. History wouldn't miss his last twenty years.

She set up the GPS co-ordinates and adjusted the

calendar and clock for her intended arrival, then hit the button that would put the machine on standby. She had settled on the night before he had first abused her – she remembered that he had been out at someone's birthday party and hadn't arrived home until gone midnight, slightly drunk and singing some crappy old pop song from the fifties, something by Buddy Holly.

She stepped into the transport cage, locked the door and strapped herself into one of the seats. According to the GPS, the cage would materialise in her old back garden, just behind the shed. It wouldn't be seen. She took a deep breath and used the remote control to initiate the jump.

The room outside the cage dissolved into deep blackness. For an instant she was frozen – in the transit period there was no way to tell if that took just a second or thousands of years, as all biological and mechanical processes within the cage were suspended – the only things that worked were the temporal flux units at each of the cages eight corners. When she could move again, she could see her family's garden through the mesh. She freed herself from the seat, slid back the cage door, and walked out into 1995.

The emergency key was in its usual place, beneath a loose flagstone weighed down with a flowerpot, just by the shed door. As quietly as she could, she unlocked the front door and entered the darkened house. She heard her mother snoring upstairs. The living room clock said it was a couple of minutes past twelve. She crept upstairs and opened her old bedroom door.

There she was, sound asleep, only her short blonde

hair and one hand visible outside the duvet. Seeing that happy and innocent child only strengthened her resolve. She would save that little girl – save herself – from years of torment and a lifetime of unhappiness. She closed the door and went downstairs to wait for her grandfather.

At twelve thirty, she heard his key scraping around the lock. He was singing 'Peggy Sue' in a slurred, tuneless voice. Eventually he got the key into the lock and reeled inside. He didn't seem surprised to see her sitting in an armchair. The alcohol must have seriously dulled his senses. He didn't speak. He merely stood there, swaying, waiting for an explanation. She rose and walked up to him, so close she could feel his beery breath on her face. It was funny – he looked much younger than she remembered. But then, all adults look really old when you're little.

'Hello Grandad,' she whispered.

He looked puzzled. 'Grandad? What the fuck are you talking about? Who are you? What are you doing in my house?'

She smiled sweetly at him then without warning hit him hard on the side of the head with the brick she had collected from the garden. He fell to the carpet. Then she hit him again and again. He didn't make a sound as he died – the only noise was that of the brick repeatedly impacting on his head. She stood over his body, panting triumphantly. Then she dropped the bloodied brick and left the house.

Back in 2017, she felt strangely disappointed. Although she had prevented the sexual abuse that had blighted her life she didn't feel any different. She still had all those bad memories, and the tension and bitterness remained. And now she actually felt guilty. She had taken her grandfather's life. But it was too late now. Sighing, she closed down the AcMe TM and erased the computer record of her trip. No one would ever know – she'd only been away for two minutes. She scribbled a note to let the Director know that she was feeling unwell and was going home.

Her mother was sitting in front of the television, glued to a daytime soap as usual. She gave her mother the customary hug and a kiss on the cheek, which went unreturned as always; then she went upstairs to lie down. As she was passing her grandfather's room, she heard snoring. Puzzled, she opened the door a crack and peered inside. The old man was stretched out on the bed, wearing just a vest and pants, sleeping soundly and noisily but still alive. Stunned, she closed the door and slid down onto the carpet in a dead faint.

Back in 2017, she was frightened. She hadn't been able to prevent her grandfather's death after all, but had seen his killer's face. It had been her own face she had seen through the living room window, her hand wielding the brick that had beaten Grandad's head to a pulp. It had been her body, wearing the clothes she had on now. What was happening? Who was that person with her face? She would never harm her grandfather, who she had loved dearly until he had been murdered by an intruder shortly after her eighth birthday. She should have stopped it, instead of just standing there, shocked beyond belief. But it was too late now. Sighing, she closed down the AcMe TM and erased the computer record of her trip. No one would ever know – she'd only been away for two minutes. She scribbled a note to let the

Director know that she was feeling unwell and was going home.

The old house was still empty and silent. She missed the sight of her mother sitting in front of the television, glued to daytime soaps. She even missed those hugs and kisses that had never been returned. Her mother had never recovered from Grandad's death and had gone into a long and steep mental decline, ultimately succumbing to an overdose of tranquillisers and sleeping tablets four years ago. Sad and still alone, she went upstairs to lie down. When she passed her grandfather's old room, she opened the door a crack and peered inside. It was still empty.

The Ray

I remember it so well, a hot, clear Sunday afternoon in the August of 1970 – not a cloud in the sky and not a care in the world. A small group of us went down to the Old Town armed with snacks and bottles of beer and wine. We sat on the bank between the beach and the footpath, near where members of the yacht club kept their boats. The wine flowed and so did the talk. In those days – we boys were only sixteen, the girls a year younger – our conversation tended to be a bit silly, though laced with occasional bolts of what seemed searing profundity and eye-widening meaning. It was that time of our lives, and that time of the world, when tiny things could assume vast significance, while the big picture eluded us almost completely. We sat and laughed and talked of nothing much and thought it was everything.

This particular afternoon was strange: sound was muted and the colours, even taking into account the blazing sunshine and bright summer clothing some of us wore, were vivid and alive. It was as though something of magnificent and possibly terrifying import was about to happen, as if the world was holding its breath and building itself up to a convulsive moment of change. Gulls wheeled and shrieked overhead like sardonic angels but even they could not break the odd mood.

Julie and I sat, both slightly drunk and very contented, talking now and then. We held hands and kissed and generally acted with the unseeing ignorance of a young couple. I looked around at Nick and Charlotte, smooching and whispering sweet nothings beneath an upturned boat; Tom and Patrick were fooling around by the water. These were my dearest friends, friends I had once only ever dreamed of having. In that moment, I loved them all fiercely and without qualification, and I knew that I would willingly and happily die for all or any one of them. As I said, I was drunk.

After a time some other people we knew came along and joined us. I can't remember who they were – they were dull pebbles compared to the brilliant jewels I was already with – though I do know that a couple of them were girls Julie and Charlotte went to school with. We drank some more, shared our cigarettes, and fooled around like the bunch of happy, carefree kids we were. Shells, sand and bewildered crabs found their way down the backs of people's jeans and into cleavages, jokes and friendly insults were traded. Tom and Patrick were helpless with mirth. The drink kept flowing.

Julie suggested a walk out to the Ray – a kind of submerged river that only appeared in the Thames when the tide was out. It was about half a mile away across the mudflats, just about visible from where we sat. Only Charlotte, her best friend, took her up on it. Nick announced that he was off to the kiosk by the quay to get some more cigarettes. The rest of us simply sat in the sun and relaxed while the girls walked out barefoot across the mud. Julie was slim and petite, with blonde hair in a ponytail; Charlotte was slightly taller, curvaceous and crowned with cascading auburn hair – so unalike physically, yet they could have been sisters. They went well together. On that day, they were like two characters from a fairytale, marching bravely out to confront a watery serpent.

I watched them as they walked out. For some reason I was entranced by the tracks they left in the mud. I could hear their cheerful talk and laughter drifting back – by some freak of acoustics it sounded like they were right next to me. I wondered if I should be worried for their safety, as the river bed was notoriously treacherous; and I briefly entertained the uncomfortable notion that they would be in real trouble if the tide came in suddenly. People had drowned out there. I don't think any of us knew when the tide was due back in. But these were fleeting anxieties. I was watching the girls walking across the mud, listening to the music of their voices and fixated on their footprints. It seemed to me that it was the most beautiful sight I had ever seen.

Hard on the heels of that thought was another revelation – that, as much as Julie and I clearly cared for each other, as close as we were, our romance wouldn't last much longer. It was affection and a strong friendship but it wasn't love. I knew we were inexplicably and tightly linked, that we would remain good friends, that we might even get together again some day, but I knew in that moment of fearsome clarity that we belonged apart as much as we belonged together. I loved her as much as I loved everyone in our little group – but no more than that. Her walk out to the Ray encapsulated the certainty of that future. It wasn't an unhappy prospect. I was sixteen years old, floating on a euphoric cocktail of hormones and alcohol, mellowed by sunshine and warmth; my senses expanded by that strange ambience. I knew there would be more to come in my life, just as there would be more to come in hers.

I watched the girls walk out to the Ray, laughed with them as they splashed around and screamed with delight, and felt grateful to the universe for granting me that single glimpse of utter perfection. But I knew that something had altered, irrevocably and permanently. With that realisation, the mood of the day changed. The universe exhaled. The clouds began to gather.

In the years since then I have often remembered that day and contemplated just what it was that I was shown. My predictions were accurate enough: we had some more good times but had drifted apart by the end of September. We went out again a couple of years later, for a few months, and parted as amicably as before. Julie married and divorced, disappeared for a while, then turned up again a few years after that, when we came close to moving in together, though somehow it didn't happen. After another couple of years she turned up again and we nearly had another little fling. The last I heard of her she was sharing a flat with Charlotte somewhere in London. That was in 1980. I do know that Charlotte married a wealthy man, someone in the media, and went to live abroad – the grapevine reaches even here, sometimes – but never found out what became of Julie. Did she find someone else? Is she happy and fulfilled? Is she still alive and in good health?

We're a long way apart now, in time if not in space, and mutual friends have moved on, died or simply lost touch. I have no way of finding out.

The times we got together after that first summer were strange and unreal, like colourless shades of our original romance. It could be argued that our summer had been so glorious, culminating in that one perfect day by the waterside, that we could never repeat it. Perhaps for us it just couldn't be equalled, though as an individual I personally had much brighter things in store. But there's something else.

Try as I might, I can only remember watching them walk out to the Ray. I have no memory of watching them come back. All I can see in my mind's eye is those tracks in the mud leading out, but none returning. I don't remember greeting her with a kiss or walking home with her afterward – the things I would normally have done. I'm known among my friends as someone with an excellent memory, and in some respects I serve as a kind of unofficial archive, remembering our shared past vividly and in detail where others have only gaps. But this has always defeated me. The last thing I can recollect with any clarity is the sight of Julie and Charlotte standing together, frozen into a tableau, out by that silvery-grey serpent winding into the estuary, dozens of gulls wheeling and shrieking over their heads. After that the day is a blank.

And maybe that's the clue to the lack of substance to those later, more shadowy times that seemed more like faded dreams even as they were happening. It is almost as if, when Julie walked out to the Ray that afternoon, she never came back at all.

Companions

'I don't remember that at all,' he said, looking out of the window at a car park.

Well, you wouldn't, would you? You were always pissed when you came here, weren't you? And since you left town you've been pissed a lot. I'm surprised you can remember your own name half the time.

It was a fair point. But right then he was painfully sober. He wished he was already several sheets to the wind, like the old boy sitting at the next table, though the sun had barely risen above the yard-arm.

'Shut up and get the drinks in.'

His companion did as instructed and went to the bar, buying two pints of Stella and carrying them carefully back to the table, which was already littered with sheets of lined A4 paper, pens, and various odds and ends he'd thought might come in handy but had so far been unwanted. His companion wrinkled his nose. The lager was flatter than he would have liked it and tasted slightly too sharp.

This lager's gone off. It's bloody horrible.

'If you don't like it you can take it back and get something else. Or you can piss off and leave me alone. I don't give a shit either way.'

The beer really was terrible, though. The ambience was worse. The pub was decorated predominantly in browns and greys. It was cramped, dark and depressing. It was, come to think of it, much as it had been years ago, though now it seemed much smaller.

They sat in silence for a while. The ingrate supped more of the beer. He wasn't bothered about the taste, not really. A pint in the hand is worth two in the barrel. He supposed he had the best of both worlds. He raised the glass at the other man, who raised his own glass in perfect synchrony and with equal irony. Mirrors tend to do exactly as they are told.

This beer tastes worse than horse-piss.

This time he didn't bother replying to himself. He was beginning to wonder why he was there, why he was waiting. He was bored and feeling lonely. The other customers were wrapped up in their own lives, and not at all interested in him. The bar staff didn't seem interested in anything at all. The image in the mirror was no company whatsoever. The man felt more kinship with the fly circling his table.

He shook his head and yearned for the days before the smoking ban, when he could have simply lit a fag to relieve the tension and tedium. This place didn't have a beer garden where he could smoke, and there was a sign instructing the clientele not to take glasses into the street outside. Why in God's name had he come here?

You're here because this is where you met her.

'When I want your opinion, I'll ask for it,' he growled.

He finished his pint and gathered his belongings from the table, stuffing them into a bag, and went to take a leak. The toilets were nicer than he remembered, but then an open cesspit would have been an improvement on the old days' lavatory facilities. As he was ascending the staircase from the subterranean toilets, he glanced out of a window and discovered that there was a beer garden after all. It was, he reflected ruefully, a bit bloody late. Nodding to the apathetic barman, who ignored him, he left the gloomy pub and walked blinking into bright sunlight.

The old town had changed a lot and there was no one he recognised, no one who knew him. He may as well have been a stranger. Actually, he realised, that was precisely what he was. After a thirty year absence he no longer had any right to call it his home town. But he didn't belong in the place he had come from that morning, either. He didn't belong anywhere, not anymore. Family, friends and lovers – one way or another all had gone. He had no home to go to, nowhere to hide.

It was no wonder he'd ended up talking to his own reflection in a mirror on a pub wall. It was even less wonder that the conversation had been fractious and sour. He hated himself, mostly because he had been right. Almost everything precious that might have existed in his head had been obliterated by years of booze and chemical indulgence. He'd tried for so long to blot things out, and now that he hoped he hadn't he found that he'd succeeded after all. He couldn't remember a bloody thing about far too many things. But there was one thing he would never forget.

The High Street was an unknown country. The shops had all changed hands, the cinema had gone, and the old flower beds were nowhere to be seen. A ghastly modernistic university had appeared in the town centre, as if dropped from the sky. The crowds were anonymous, generic town centre masses indistinguishable from any other. He sat in a seat by a pavement café and rolled a cigarette. A bad-tempered young woman in a striped uniform and appallingly cheerful corporate hat told him to buy something or clear off. He chose the latter option.

This was no longer his place. It hadn't been his home for many years. It was as if the locals could sense it. Their hostility and resentment were the same as they would hold for any interloper. He was an invasive organism, a virus. He was a foreign body and his home town was finally rejecting him. Everyone he met was an antibody.

On the seafront, things were no better, though the air seemed fresher and the people happier. They were nearly all tourists, he realised. To them this was nothing more than a pleasant day out by the seaside. Many of them were slightly drunk. He envied them, but those hedonistic days were behind him; as were all the others. Like the elephants of popular imagination, he had come home to die. He wished he had been born somewhere nicer. He sat on the sea wall and had another smoke.

Why are you thinking like this? You're not even sixty. You're still relatively young and there's nothing wrong with you, as far as you know. Why are you so determined to die?

'Everyone dies eventually,' he told himself. 'It's my time. Enough is enough.'

You're such a loser.

He threw the browned, soggy cigarette-butt to the ground and stamped on it. On the way back to the High Street he spotted a litter bin and began extracting unused items from his bag and throwing them away. Then he gave up sorting through his stuff and dumped the entire bag and its contents into the receptacle. All he kept were his tobacco pouch and wallet. He wished he could get rid of his clothes too, but the last thing he needed was a night in the cells for a display of public indecency. That would interfere with his plan.

Shorn of all but comforting nicotine, a little money and an identity, he continued on his way, back into the High Street and to a side-road where a café used to be. The café, once owned by an Italian family who also made excellent ice-cream, was now a Costa. He went in anyway and spent the last of his money on a large Americano. The coffee was much better than it used to be but he missed the old place. He remembered that one of his friends had gone out with a woman who worked there, and they would often feast on unsold food that would otherwise have been discarded. He wondered what had become of the woman. His friend, he knew, had become seriously religious and ran a website that issued increasingly demented warnings of the Final Days and promised eternal damnation for Godless sinners. The man he remembered from the old days had been a hard-drinking, sulphate-snorting punk rock fan. A poacher turned gamekeeper. It was a common transformation.

With the cash gone and the coffee finished, he opened his tobacco pouch and rolled one for the road. He lit up inside the Costa, sparking protests from another customer, and walked out leaving the pouch on the table. There was enough tobacco left for a few cigarettes. Someone else could have the benefit. He smoked the cigarette on the way to the station, relishing every drag.

In the station toilet he relieved himself of the last of

the beer and the first of the coffee then removed everything from his wallet except his return ticket. He had no intention of returning but the ticket was essential. Catching sight of his reflection in a stained and pitted mirror, he paused to inspect himself. Grey hair, spectacles, and a paunch that had diminished of late but was still unsightly. He was dressed all in black. That was pleasing. Without realising it he had dressed for the occasion.

Who are you kidding? You'll never go through with it.

'You don't know me as well as you think. You have no idea what I could or couldn't do.'

I know you well enough to be able to tell you to your face that you're a coward and a loser.

'It's none of your damned business. Anyway, what's with all the concern? You never cared before. You were never around when I needed you. You were never there when I needed someone to talk to, when I needed a friend. You only ever show up when you want to prove a point.'

You mustn't do it. What about all the people you'll leave behind? They'll be hurt and upset. Don't do it to them.

'What people? My friends have all either died or gone away and can't be traced. My family are either gone or they're not people I would care to know. There's no one else except a few people at work who barely acknowledge my existence. Nobody will give a damn.'

Well, at least keep the wallet. If you do this you'll be a real mess. Don't make life any tougher for the poor buggers who have to scrape you up by making them work to identify you.

He hesitated. His companion had a point. He was a tired man but not a cruel one. Finally, he thought of a compromise. He removed the cards and put them in his pocket, and left the empty wallet by the hand basin.

On the platform he stood close to the yellow line and waited. He heard the rails sing as a train approached and moved a little nearer to the edge. Not long to wait, maybe less than a minute.

Please don't do it.

'Give me one good reason why not,' he retorted, his eyes fixed on the point where he would aim the leap that would never be completed.

If you do this it will be gone forever. That one golden moment that you cherish will be gone. You're the only one who remembers it now. When you're gone that will go too, and no one will ever know. It will be as if it never happened. That one golden moment – isn't that worth being remembered by someone?

The lines were singing louder and he could hear wheels grinding, steel against steel. He readied himself for the leap to nowhere.

'Not good enough,' he said.

But you can remember that, can't you? You remember what she was like – her hair, her eyes, and the way she smiled and laughed. You remember the feel of her skin and the softness and warmth that made you want to fly like a bird. You can remember her voice, the way she moved, how it felt when she was in your arms. And I know you remember what she said to you that day, those words that made you feel more alive than you'd ever felt before.

He closed his eyes. It was seconds away now.

'She's gone,' he whispered emptily, and readied himself to take that final flight as the train approached. 'She's gone forever.'

Not while you remember.

He made ready to jump.

Not while you remember.

I bet you're glad you took my advice and kept the cards.

'Yeah, and now I have to buy more tobacco and a new bloody wallet. And I threw my keys away so I'm locked out. You always get me with that one. One of these days I'm going to have a good answer.'

At least you don't have to fork out for a new ticket. And you won't be able to smoke anyway, not until you get to the other end.

'You mean until I get back to mundane misery and pointlessness. I have so much to thank you for.'

Sarcasm is the lowest form of wit, you know.

'It's all you're getting from me, so be bloody grateful. Now I have to get through the rest of the day somehow. Thanks for nothing.'

Every year you come back here, on the anniversary of her death, to the place where she died. You feel guilty, as if you were somehow to blame. But it was an accident. There were witnesses who saw it all. It was even caught on CCTV. She tripped over her own feet and fell. There was nothing anyone could have done.

'But I was supposed to be with her that day. She wanted to go shopping in the West End but I cried off because I wanted to go to a fucking football match with my mates, for God's sake. If I'd been there I might have been able to save her.'

And you know damned well that you wouldn't have been quick enough to stop her going over the edge and in front of that train. Look, we've had the same conversation on the same day every year for more than thirty years. It always ends the same way. Why do you keep doing it?

'You know why. I do it because it's the only way I can

think of her like that without the pain, thinking I will be with her soon, wherever she is. It's the only time I ever have any feeling of hope, any sense that there might be something better.'

But you're always saying every day might be the last, that death can strike anyone, at any time. You never know what's just around the corner. You tell people they should live by those sentiments. Why can't you take your own advice and treat every day as if it might be your last?

'In case it isn't,' he said. 'In case it isn't.'

They were silent for a while, the man and his reflection in the train lavatory compartment's mirror. After a while they sighed and finished washing their hands.

So, same time next year then?

'Yeah, same time next year.'

The Devil's Verse

He'd laboured for long hours and it was still imperfect. Now, staring down at the spidery words on that coffee-stained sheet of paper, he wondered why he bothered. Yes, his fellow practitioners said his work was good – better than good, Sandeman had told him, a distinctly green hue to his eyes – and almost everything he submitted to magazines and journals appeared in print. Sometimes he even liked what he'd done – but only up to a point. The truth was that the more he read his own poems, the worse he thought they were. And this latest one – this one bloody piece that was so important, the one he planned to submit to the *Observer* poetry competition – was simply terrible.

Angrily, he crumpled the paper into a rough sphere and threw it toward the waste-paper basket in the corner of his room. The missile fell short and joined its six partners in failure on the faded burgundy carpet. He stared at it impassively for a few seconds then took another sheet of paper from a desk drawer. He refilled his gold-nibbed fountain pen and tried to rethink the verse. The choice of writing implement was, he freely admitted, pretentious but he firmly believed that a poet used beauty to create beauty, and the elegant pen seemed to be just the right thing for that snowy, virginal paper. It was just a pity that everything they produced was so bloody bad. He grudgingly admitted that he quite liked his poems but that wasn't the same as agreeing that they were good. He wrote because he loved doing it. He had no burning desire to prove he was any better than anyone else. He only submitted his poems for publication when Sandeman talked him into it, usually when they were drinking. And now Sandeman had talked him into entering the damned competition.

Just as he was about to inscribe the first letter of the opening word for the umpteenth time, the telephone rang, fracturing his concentration. Oh well, it didn't matter. The mood was clearly next to useless anyway. With a heavy sigh that was as much of relief as frustration, he lifted the receiver.

It was Sandeman, asking to meet him in the pub an hour earlier than usual. There was someone who wanted to meet him. Sandeman wouldn't be drawn on the nature of this person but evidently thought it was important. Reluctantly, O'Keefe agreed. With his poetic faculties in a state of disarray bordering on outright and ignominious retreat, a few drinks before the poetry club meeting would probably be for the best. Embarrassment is so much easier to take when one is slightly drunk.

Michael O'Keefe belonged to a small group of poets who called themselves Poetic Licentiousness. They specialised in mildly erotic verse that echoed Baudelaire, Rimbaud and Verlaine, with absent-minded nods to Mallarmé, Poe and Wilde. Fashionably old-fashioned, they celebrated looking backward as if through a glass darkly. Heavy on symbolism, despairing sighs and wicked romance, their creations were redolent of the rainforest and the graveyard as much as the boudoir and the brasserie. They stank of opium and absinthe, hashish and rose-water. The modern world was only allowed to enter their creativity at the point where the technological age began. Word documents, keyboards and LCD monitors were *verboten*; though they could be used to transcribe verse for submission to magazines. Otherwise it was pen and paper all the way through composition and revision to that first reading that announced perfection. That was the golden rule.

The strange thing was that although their verse was rooted in the decades before the end of the Victorian era, the poems were surprising popular and seemingly relevant to the early twenty-first century. Post-modern irony didn't come into it – the *oeuvre* of Poetic Licentiousness was densely symbolic and so allusional as to be virtually abstract. They gave decadence a new cadence. Their work – particularly the poems of Sandeman and O'Keefe – was welcomed eagerly by editors and subscribers alike. They were discussed on the *Culture Show* and the *Late Review*, the darlings of BBC2, the broadsheets and the chattering class. None of them could understand it. Only Sandeman consistently had a high opinion of his own work, a fact possibly connected with his near-constant inebriation and regular forays into the world of narcotics; yet even he was baffled. Several large gins into one epic evening session he confessed 'Yes, I think my poetry is very good. But it's so bloody dated. We do it because we're fans and because we enjoy it. People should be reading modern works not our dusty old nonsense.'

Like the Symbolist and Decadent artists of the late nineteenth century, their imagery was unrestrained and wild. Romance, sex, death, madness and fury rampaged through their imaginations until it was all but impossible to tell one theme from the others. Like the Decadents, when it worked it was astonishingly powerful and evocative; but when it went badly it reeked of the charnel house, disease and venereal decay. And, like the Decadents, Satan and all his bat-winged minions were never far away.

One of the poets, a pale and somewhat wasted-looking young man who called himself Edgar De'Ath, once claimed to have heard of something known as the Devil's Verse, a sort of poetic equivalent of the so-called 'Devil's Interval', the *diabolus in musica* that made some musical compositions profoundly unsettling. De'Ath had breathlessly told his colleagues that any poet accidentally stumbling upon this particular combination of metre, sounds and context was doomed to damnation, and would be immediately carried away by Satan and consigned to the torments of Hell. Huysmans had called it *la poésie des damnés*, according to De'Ath; while Apollinaire named it *le verset de la damnation*. The idea had been known as far back as Juvenal, for whom it was *diabolus in poetica*. Or so De'Ath said. Naturally, that had inspired them all to experiment there and then. Well, they were all very drunk at the time and it made a change from the usual melodramas in which diabolical forces were referenced frequently but never taken seriously. Fortunately, nothing had come of their attempted Satanism except some excruciatingly dreadful poems and a lot of very bad hangovers. O'Keefe suspected that De'Ath's story was as authentic as his name and thought no more of it. Sandeman, on the other hand, fuelled by gin, cocaine and those enormous cigars he liked to smoke, had thrown himself into researching the use of sound in magic and ritual – archaeo-acoustics, the Enochian language, glossolalia, Siberian shamans' songs, throat-singing, Gregorian and Tibetan chants, and the physical effects of sonic frequencies on the human nervous system. Eventually he had succumbed to the effects of prodigious quantities of drugs and booze on his own neuropsychology and spent a couple of weeks in detox, after which he forgot all about it.

During the night O'Keefe had rescued his poem from total disaster and was now almost looking forward to the evening's meeting, hopefully a slightly more sober affair than the previous gathering, which had culminated in a near-brawl between Sandeman and one of De'Ath's least tolerant friends. O'Keefe was less nervous than usual, largely because he was intrigued by the person Sandeman wanted him to meet, which was a welcome distraction. Members were allowed to bring guests to their headquarters – a shoddily-furnished room in a nearby arts centre – so presumably this mysterious person was to attend as Sandeman's guest. With the poem neatly folded and safe in the inside pocket of his jacket, O'Keefe entered the pub and scanned the bar for his friend.

To his surprise, Sandeman – in his familiar black *sombrero cordobés* and opera cape – was with a woman. And not just any woman; she was entrancingly beautiful, drop-dead gorgeous in the hateful modern parlance, though even 'hot' sprang to O'Keefe's mind as he studied her from what he considered the safest distance to get a good look without being scorched. She was around thirty, with long, jet-black hair and sultry brown eyes that seemed to promise an awful lot of things O'Keefe had only read or dreamed guiltily about. As for her figure – O'Keefe wished he had a mitre and a stained-glass window handy. She was dressed all in black and purple, the style known as 'goth' but which was as decadent as he could have wished for.

He sat heavily in the vacant chair between Sandeman and the woman. Sandeman introduced them and swayed to the bar to get O'Keefe a vodka and bitter lemon, and to top up his own gin and tonic. The woman smiled knowingly.

'You didn't catch my name, did you?'

'No,' said O'Keefe, slightly embarrassed. He had been too busy trying to recover from the sight of her to hear whatever Sandeman had said. 'I'm afraid I was a bit distracted. I'm Michael O'Keefe.'

'You can call me Thérèse,' she told him. 'It's not my real name but that's too ordinary for words. Do you read Zola?'

'I'm not one for novels, really. I tend to read poetry and books about art and history.'

'That's a pity. Zola's very good but a bit moralistic. I took my name from one of his books. I wanted to redeem the character, free her from guilt, remorse and shame. I'm married, just like her, but I follow my passions and do what I want to do. My husband knows -- but he understands my terms. Everything's a compromise and that's his. My compromise is – well, that would be telling.'

Uncomfortable at this semi-candour, O'Keefe prayed for Sandeman to return from the bar. A quick glance informed him that Sandeman had been sidetracked by one of their fellows, none other than Edgar De'Ath. O'Keefe was on his own in *terra incognita*. He swallowed hard and gamely attempted to act normally.

'Sandeman said you wanted to meet me.'

'Yes. I wanted to meet the man responsible for those amazing poems. I find them incredibly erotic, very sensual and arousing. I wanted to see if the poet measured up to the verse.'

'And do I?' O'Keefe was almost in a panic. Thérèse was leaning close to him and her perfume was as overpowering as the proximity of those fabulous breasts and those inviting lips.

She was amused. 'I don't know yet,' she stage-whispered. 'I think it'll take more than one meeting to get to the bottom of you. I'd like to meet you in more intimate surroundings.'

O'Keefe was saved from exploding by the return of Sandeman, who drunkenly steered the conversation into safer waters – in other words, he started talking loudly about his favourite subject, namely himself.

The rest of the evening was a blur. O'Keefe's poem was well-received, though he barely noticed. All he could think about was the luscious, intoxicating Thérèse. At around nine o'clock he noticed that she had disappeared. He was both greatly relieved and crushingly disappointed. He had been half-hoping for an invitation to those more intimate surroundings she had mentioned. Now that she had gone, he conveniently ignored the fact that the fraction of hope had been matched by an equal proportion of fear. Consequently the relief dwindled to nothing and all he felt was regret.

That night, first he was unable to sleep – several large vodkas had no sedative value – then, when sleep did come, his dreams were lurid, turbulent fantasies owing more to Keats and Coleridge than his more recent heroes, filled with images of Thérèse. She appeared as Lamia, La Belle Dame Sans Merci and the Nightmare Life-in-Death, with the pale skin, raven locks and scarlet lips of a vampire. She was a doomed Pre-Raphaelite consumptive, eyes fever-hot and shining wetly in a waxen face; a razor-toothed *Arabian Nights* demoness; and a curiously demure Whore of Babylon riding in deadly triumph upon a seven-headed dragon. Then she was Moreau's Salomé, dancing voluptuous and naked but for tattoos adorning her flesh like a skein of translucent jewels, gloating over O'Keefe's severed head on a bloody silver platter. At least that was more familiar territory. But when he awoke, sweating and breathing hard with arousal and dread, O'Keefe knew that the stylistic confusion meant only one thing. He was wholly besotted, utterly terrified and was ransacking his subconscious for images that suited her. The woman was a demon and he was possessed. He was certain he was in mortal peril. He had to see her again, the sooner the better.

Sandeman wasn't too pleased at the early morning telephone call. He was feeling delicate after the night's excesses, which had continued long after the Poetic Licentiousness meeting had ended and the pub had closed, and seemed to have involved a large amount of marijuana and a few lines of cocaine on top of the gin he had consumed. He remembered introducing O'Keefe to Thérèse, and even claimed to recall O'Keefe's poem. But he knew nothing about the woman. She had collared Sandeman in another pub a few evenings previously after being told by someone who knew someone else that Sandeman could help her meet O'Keefe. He had arranged to meet her shortly before the meeting and had exchanged only a few polite words with her prior to O'Keefe's arrival.

'I thought she was just another poetry groupie,' said Sandeman defensively. 'You know what people are like.'

Poetry groupies? That was the first O'Keefe had heard of such a thing. He knew pop stars had them, and there were many well-known instances of women becoming romantically involved with poets and novelists – but poetry groupies? He had a momentary vision of himself in a dressing room with the door barricaded against screaming teenaged girls. No, that was ridiculous. Besides, Thérèse seemed a bit too mature and subtly sardonic to be in the grip of a hysterical infatuation. She was an experienced woman who knew what she wanted and he suspected she didn't much care how she got it and who was hurt in the process. The short conversation he'd had with her was enough to convince him that she was trouble in the making.

O'Keefe realised he didn't actually want anything to do with Thérèse. That was his survival instinct telling him to keep away. Yet he also understood that he wanted everything to do with her. That was instinct too, though this one had more to do with mating than survival. He wished he hadn't stopped smoking. He really needed a cigarette. He rummaged in his desk and found some Nicorette, popped four pieces of the gum into his mouth and chewed furiously until the nicotine began to work. Feeling a little calmer, he decided that he'd had a lucky escape. She was not the sort of person he would consider having any kind of relationship with. She was bad news and he was fortunate that she'd not been around when he'd finished reading his poem. She must have decided he came up short against his measure. He laughed aloud at his own wit and decided to make a pot of tea.

Then the telephone rang. It was Thérèse.

'Sandeman gave me your telephone number last night,' she told him. 'That poem was fabulous, really sexy. Would you like to meet me for lunch?'

He'd been seeing her for nearly three months. Sometimes he saw her for three or four days consecutively. Then he might not see her for a week, and once her absence stretched to an intolerable fortnight. Their meetings were always at her convenience – she would phone him or just turn up unheralded on his doorstep and expect admittance. He had no idea how to contact her – he didn't know her telephone number, as the caller ID was always blocked, and he didn't have the faintest idea where she lived. He didn't even know her real name. She said he didn't need to know any of those things. She would come to him, as and when she felt like it, and when she did she would be Thérèse. That would be his compromise, she'd told him. She would also compromise, just as she did in her other life. But what that compromise was would remain a secret. Those were her terms, her side of their pact. O'Keefe nervously joked that it ought to be signed in blood.

There was no pattern to her attentions. She seemed to have no interest in clocks or the diurnal cycle. Her moods were unpredictable and bewildering. The only constant was frustration. It had been three months of torture by teasing, innuendo and suggestive smiles. Thérèse touched him often – a hand on his shoulder, a light flutter of fingertips on his hand, a brief brush of lips against his cheek – but though sex seemed always to be imminent it was somehow never on her agenda. If he ever tried to touch her his hand was quickly slapped away.

She was intelligent and well-informed, with a large vocabulary, a precise yet exotically husky voice and a filthy laugh. Every time they met Thérèse insinuated that she would sleep with him soon – though her speech was so littered with double entendres that it was often difficult for O'Keefe to work out what was meant seriously and what was a actually an obscene joke. Not that he really cared. Her presence was a drug that he could never get enough of and which always left him craving more, no matter how cruel or derisive she sometimes was. He was addicted to her as surely as Sandeman was an alcoholic coke-fiend. And he was in denial, of course. He knew she was playing with him but he couldn't bring himself to face up to the truth.

Thérèse once came to his flat at two o'clock in the morning. She'd been drinking – he could smell whisky on her breath – but was still in command of herself and in absolute control of the situation. She made him take off all his clothes then performed an elaborate and protracted striptease until she was down to her undergarments. She pushed him down onto his bed, knelt astride his chest – then laughed, stood and got dressed again. Then she departed, leaving O'Keefe to his own devices. It was the most extreme of a number of ploys in which she first raised his hopes then mercilessly shattered them.

Most often she would engage him in conversation about his poetry, questioning him closely about the meaning of particular words and phrases, wanting to know why he had used one word and not another, what was in his mind and heart when he wrote, and what he was going to write next. It was bitterly ironic because he hadn't written a single damned line since he'd first laid eyes on her. The *Observer* competition seemed a distant memory, his intended entry lying dusty and forgotten on a shelf. How could he write when all he could see in his mind's eye was her face, when all he could think of was the unfulfilled promise of her body? How could he compose verse when every night was a maelstrom of torrid dreams that shaded easily into orgiastic but ultimately sterile nightmares? How could he do anything at all when he was totally obsessed with having sex with her? And when she wouldn't let him?

He stopped going to the Poetic Licentiousness meetings. He had nothing to contribute and hadn't the heart to listen to poetry when he was unable to write any of his own. He told Sandeman he was sick, first influenza then post-viral fatigue. It wasn't a very big lie, he told himself. He really was unwell – but the disease was Thérèse. And that sickness had its own complications: he didn't merely lust after her – he actually liked her. He admired her intellect and independence, and part of him genuinely found her games amusing. He appreciated the temptress for what he was, as much as he despaired at what she was doing to him.

One day O'Keefe had an idea. It was lunchtime. They were sitting in a café – he always paid, that was taken for granted – discussing poetry as usual, when it came to him.

He was electrified, unable to believe that he hadn't already thought of it.

'Would you like me to write a poem for you?'

Thérèse's melting-chocolate eyes lost focus and her face softened. 'Would you do that for me? Really? Yes, I think I'd like that very much.'

For a moment O'Keefe thought he might receive his reward for gallantry there and then. Thérèse was looking at him in a way she never had, her expression one of naked desire rather than the expected sarcastic coquettishness. Her pupils were dilated and she abruptly rearranged her body to mirror the way he was sitting. He'd read these were sure-fire indications of sexual interest. His hopes rose, and they weren't alone. Suddenly she leaned across the table, grasped his hand and stared intently into his eyes.

'How long will it take?' she asked.

'Oh, about a week, I suppose – maybe less.'

She stroked his wrist with her thumb. 'You'd write a poem, for me. That makes me feel so horny. If it's a good one I'll make sure you have a night you'll never forget. I'll see you in seven days.'

Her fingers lingered on his hand and her eyes remained fixed on his face as she stood. She turned and slowly walked out of the café, her hips swaying sinuously.

O'Keefe leaned back in his chair and tried to remember how to breathe.

At ten minutes to midnight, the poem was ready at last. O'Keefe read through it several times. It was, he thought, the best thing he'd ever written – a fevered imagining of Thérèse as a beautiful phantom, a mesmerising succubus and a goddess of delirium. It was, in effect, one of his dreams put into words and ordered in lines of blank verse with subtle internal rhymes and stresses, hidden meanings and nuances.

The effort had cost him dearly. He'd hardly eaten or slept at all since that lunchtime in the café, and he had taken up smoking again. He'd even gone so far as to scrounge some of Sandeman's seemingly endless supply of cocaine to keep him going and spark inspiration when the coffee and nicotine proved inadequate. Now he was haggard, hollow-eyed and exhausted. But he was ready. O'Keefe decided to take a shower before retiring to his bed for a good, long sleep that would restore him for when he saw Thérèse the next day, assuming she would keep her side of the bargain.

He was still towelling himself dry when she knocked on his door. She raised an eyebrow when she saw him standing there wearing only a bathrobe.

'I think you may be counting your chickens,' she said in that teasing, throaty voice.

'Sorry,' he offered, feeling awkward. 'I wasn't expecting you. I've just got out of the shower. I didn't think you'd be here so – immediately. Would you like coffee?'

'No, all I want right now is to hear you read my poem. After that – well, we'll see.'

She perched on the edge of his bed and smiled encouragingly. He swallowed and fetched the sheet of paper from his desk. It was as rumpled and coffee-stained as the last poem he'd written. He cleared his throat and began to read.

When he'd finished, she sat and stared at him in silence. She seemed subdued, disappointed. O'Keefe waited for her to speak. He jumped when she finally emitted a short bark of a laugh.

'It was all going so well until the last line,' she sighed. 'All that sublimated sex and passionate metaphor – then you ruined the whole thing.'

'I don't understand,' said O'Keefe, puzzled and hurt. 'All it said was how I feel, that I...'

She held up a warning finger. 'Don't you bloody say it again,' she said sternly. 'I never want to hear that from anyone except my husband.'

'But...'

'Listen to me, Michael. I told you that my marriage was all about compromises – my husband's compromise is that he gets me, every bit of me, as long as he lets me do what I like when he's not there. My compromise to him is that I will not become involved emotionally with anyone I may wish to sleep with. Your compromise was that you only ever got to see me on my terms, only when I was able or in the mood to see you. I told you that I compromised in return – well, it was a secret but you may as well hear it now, because nothing will ever happen between us. My compromise was that while I was seeing you – while I was deciding whether to sleep with you – I wouldn't have sex with anyone else except my husband. Then you had to spoil it all by developing bloody *feelings* for me. Why couldn't you have stuck to lust like other men?'

'But – but – I – I can't help it,' O'Keefe stammered, appalled at what she had just revealed. 'That's what poetry is all about, expressing feelings and beauty.'

Thérèse rolled her eyes and sneered. 'Not for me, it isn't. For me, poetry is about sex and death and insanity, things that astonish and amaze me, all those things you usually write about. Isn't that why you like the Decadents and the others? Because they scratch away at conventional morality and show it for the sham it is? Isn't truth the most beautiful thing of all? What you wrote isn't the truth – it's a statement of acquisition and ownership. No one *owns* me and no one *acquires* me – not even my husband, to whom I freely give my spirit and my affection. I give myself to others, but only physically and only on my terms. What you want isn't available, not from me.'

'But I...'

'No! Don't you *ever* say that to me, you poor, sad bastard. Only one person has the right to say that to me and it isn't you, Michael O'Keefe.'

She stormed out, slamming the door behind her. O'Keefe stared at the door then looked down at the sheet of paper in his hand. He felt as if his heart had been ripped from his chest and he'd been flayed alive. Nothing like it had ever happened to him before. He knew it was his own stupid fault – it had been obvious right from the start that she was playing a dangerous game and that he was ignorant of the rules. It was always going to end badly and he should have exercised proper caution. In fact, he should have avoided her like the bloody plague. But acknowledging that he had been the author of his own tragedy didn't make him feel any better. The misery was overwhelming, so intense that he knew he was going to suffer for a very long time and that it would seem like an eternity.

Trembling and shocked by what had just happened, he read through his poem again. No matter how heartfelt or well-intentioned, no matter how sincere the emotions it expressed, the cause of his destruction was there for anyone to see, for everyone to hear. De'Ath had been right. It didn't matter whether or not it really had been known to Huysmans, Apollinaire, Juvenal or anyone else – the poetry of damnation, the Devil's Verse, was real. He hadn't realised that it consisted of just a single word to the wrong person. Hell was always only one syllable away. And the Devil had been there all along, waiting in his heart like a worm in a blighted bud.

L'Histoire Perdue

Nothing much works here anymore. I have gas and electricity but the light switches are broken and the bulbs have all blown. I have neither the money nor the energy to replace them. There is a cooker, a washing machine and a refrigerator but they may as well be somewhere else. Now and then they creak or wheeze into a kind of life but it's usually not for very long. I wash my clothes in the bath and keep my perishable foods in sealed plastic bags immersed in cold water. There's always plenty of cold water because the boiler doesn't work. The radio is jammed on a setting that picks up only static and distorted music from a nearby Asian pirate station, Bollywood show-tunes and bhangra beats, someone speaking Hindi or Urdu or some other language I don't know. The neighbours are quiet, which is a blessing.

The telephone is fine but nobody calls me and I have no one to call. The television also works; but there's nothing to watch but reality and game shows, celebrity this and that, soap operas, cooking and home makeovers, and idiots displaying their most intimate medical anxieties. The computer works sometimes but the software is always playing up and internet connection is intermittent because the wireless signal keeps dropping out. It's enough for my needs.

I live in silence and candlelight. I read and think and write with few distractions. I almost like it that way. The flickering flames soothe me when I am troubled, which is often. The quiet is beautiful and terrible.

Every once in a while I feel the need to go out and seek company. It isn't often, perhaps once a month. When that urge takes me I don't go far, a short walk to the nearest pub. I know people there, some people who are sometimes there. We've never spoken but I know them. I buy a beer, something light and cold, and sit and listen to them talking and float away with the voices. Sometimes from the corner of my eye I see those waves of rippling colour, though I always ignore them. Then I go home to the place where nothing much works.

The first time it happened I was seventeen, out with my friends from school, messing about and wasting time the way kids do. It was a sunny day with a smell of approaching rain, warm and humid. I think it was June. We were in the park, kicking a tennis ball around because we had no money and nothing else to do. It wasn't a proper game of anything, just kicking it to each other, sometimes picking it up and throwing it. One of my friends, I can't remember who it was, threw it high into the air above me. I looked up to try to see it against the sun. Suddenly there was lightning, multicoloured flashes and streaks all around me. Then I heard singing, a heavenly choir like the ones in those corny films when people die and go to heaven. After that I wasn't there anymore.

When I could see and hear and think again there was a crowd of people around me. My friends looked scared. A couple of adults – a couple, a man and a woman maybe forty years old – were kneeling beside me, asking if I was alright. I don't remember doing or saying anything. An ambulance arrived and I was put on a stretcher and taken to hospital. I was examined by two doctors and looked after by a nurse who didn't look much older than me. She was nice-looking and very kind. I was still dazed and beginning to be a little afraid, or I might have done something stupid like ask her for a date. I was full of myself in those days. Until then, that is.

The doctors couldn't find anything wrong with me. My mother and father had arrived by the time they were ready to confess their lack of conclusions. It was just as well because I wasn't taking anything in. All I could think about was that nurse. I didn't really fancy her, that's the thing. She was sweet and pretty but that wasn't it. No, it was because whenever I looked at her I saw a halo around her, a beautiful silvery glow, a nimbus like something from an old religious painting. It was breathtaking.

An appointment was made for more tests and my parents took me home in a taxi. The doctors, I was told later, had suggested that it might be something as innocuous as my blood-sugar levels dropping sharply because I'd been running around and sweating in that heat and humidity. But they warned us it might be epilepsy. Apparently I hadn't had convulsions or a fit or anything like that. I'd simply stood absolutely still for a full minute while my friends yelled at me, asking me what was wrong; then

I'd dropped to the ground and lay there, unmoving, while the passers-by stopped to help and one of my worried friends had gone to phone for an ambulance.

And that was my first time. It happened regularly after that, once every couple of months, sometimes more frequently. It was always different, though, every time. The second time it happened I awoke from my seizure, or whatever it was, speaking French. It was Sunday dinner-time and we'd been sitting round the table getting stuck into roast beef, potatoes and Yorkshire pudding before I wound up on the floor, next to my dinner. *Cherchez l'histoire perdue*, I said to my astonished parents. *Ma vie en dépend.* My eyes, I was told, were wide and afraid; my voice urgent. *Look for the lost story, my life depends on it.*

They called an ambulance and again I was examined and tested; and again I was pronounced puzzlingly well. But this time my parents were convinced that whatever had happened was no mere medical crisis. I took German in secondary school. I neither speak nor understand French. My mother did, and she was astonished at my unexpected and baffling facility with the language. The doctors agreed that it was unusual, but apparently it was not unusual enough. Although I had once again failed to present symptoms consistent with epilepsy, they announced that I must have suffered a grand mal seizure. The additional tests were brought forward.

Two months later I found myself wearing a hospital gown, wired up to an electro-encephalograph. In the interim I had experienced a further episode in which I found myself lying in the street with the fading image of a vast cloud of brightly-coloured feathers wheeling around my head. No one else noticed anything unusual. I had been afraid, yet felt calm. The fear was more conceptual than actual.

During the test my brain decided to put on a show for the specialists. The celestial chorale and technicolour lightshow came, and I left temporarily for somewhere else, somewhere I never remembered but thought might be a very long way from that hospital room. There were no convulsions. There was no abnormal brain activity. My pulse maintained a stead sixty-five beats a minute, and my blood pressure was seemingly unaffected. Blood-sugar levels were normal when tested. Respiration was shallow but normal, as if I were merely asleep or resting. My reflexes were fine and my eyes reacted normally when a light was shone in them. Physically, the only sign that something might be amiss was my utter stillness and the fact that I did not respond to questioning, poking or prodding. But in the few minutes after I came out of my trance I appeared slightly confused and surprised to be back; and I was speaking French again. *J'ai envie de voir l'ange de l'arc en ciel. Elle connaît l'histoire perdue. Ma vie ne vaut rien sans l'histoire.* This time it was a doctor who translated. *I want to see the rainbow angel. She knows the lost story. My life is worthless without the story.*

Now the absence of symptoms convinced the doctors that I was indeed experiencing epileptic seizures, and that I must have some undetectable cerebral anomaly, probably in one of my temporal lobes. They told my parents I would have to take medication to keep it under control. They prescribed a drug called carbamazepine.

I dutifully took the drug. I daresay it worked well enough for other people but for me it had side effects. I developed rashes and nausea, and had severe mood swings. I became depressed, so depressed that on several occasions I seriously contemplated suicide. When I saw the doctors about these, they merely adjusted the dosage, usually upward. The side effects worsened. The doctors blamed the array of new symptoms on my phantom epilepsy. I dropped out of school, unable to focus on my A-levels. Morose and occasionally unexpectedly aggressive, I lost friends. One by one they drifted away until I had none. The medication didn't stop the strange episodes. But it stopped everything else.

Exactly one year after I started taking the medication, I decided enough was enough and flushed the medication down the toilet. What was the use of taking drugs that made me feel so bad when they didn't even do what they were supposed to do? I had a few very rough weeks – they never told me that like diazepam this drug was addictive and would result in severe withdrawal symptoms if I abruptly stopped taking it – but I rode out the appalling discomfort and it wasn't too long before I became a little more like my old self. Except for those strange ecstasies, of course. I still spoke French sometimes, when I was returning to reality, but it was always a variation on those first two utterances.

I didn't get my old friends back. They no longer trusted me to be either civil or non-aggressive. I couldn't blame them, not really. I'd probably have felt the same way if it had been one of them. It was disappointing, though in all honesty I couldn't even work out if they had shown me too little loyalty or just had it driven out of them by the way I'd behaved while under the influence of the carbamazepine. I supposed there was only so much of me anyone could take.

By then I'd been out of school for over a year and had never had a job. All I could get after that was unskilled labour or low-grade clerical work. My fistful of O-levels didn't seem to count for much in the job market, save to distinguish me from the complete no-hopers – a distinction nullified by my neurology. The medical history didn't exactly help, and I lost several jobs when I suddenly took an excursion to nowhere in the middle of an office or on a factory floor. The condition wasn't in itself a reason to sack me, but because of it they always found other reasons. My employment record was peppered with employers' lies and latticed with lacunae.

Another year had passed when I had the idea that perhaps I was trying to tell myself something. *L'histoire perdue* – the lost story. Was I telling myself that I should become a writer? I had never been very good at writing stories when I was younger, but what you can do at twenty should be bit more than you could do when you were seventeen or younger. I gave it a try. I converted some of my Supplementary Benefit into a couple of narrow feint A4 notepads and a dozen black ballpoint pens. Then I locked myself away – which was really only closing my bedroom door – and tried to write a novel. I was thinking big. Perhaps it would change my life, make me some money and new friends, and help me out of the rut I was in. It was going to be about a failed actor who made a living from television commercials and would be called *Short Shows*.

Six months later, all I had was a solitary sheet of paper with only the title written at the top, a couple of crossed-out first lines, and some doodles. I forced myself to face the facts. I didn't have a single idea in my head. Whatever mechanism writers had in their minds that allowed them to write, I didn't have it. I used the notepads to make lists, lists of everything. I began with my hundred favourite books, hoping that might inspire me to write. It didn't. I moved on to my hundred favourite songs, then albums, then television programmes, places, people, animals – you name it and I made a list of my hundred favourites. They didn't turn into a work of fiction. Later, I tried something else. I saved up my benefit and bought a cheap acoustic guitar from a second-hand shop, along with a tutorial by Bert Weedon. But I was useless – no co-ordination, no feel for it at all. At least I recouped some of my cash when I sold them back to the shop. After that I tried writing poetry but once again came up empty-handed as far as ideas were concerned.

I had no discernible talent for anything except falling into strange trances and speaking in French about rainbow angels and lost stories. I resigned myself to a life of menial work and tedious drudgery. Then came the Thatcher years and even unskilled employment dried up. At twenty-five years old my life ground to a halt.

That was when I saw her. It was the November of 1979 and I was sitting in a café drinking coffee. She walked in with a friend, laughing at a remark the other woman had made. I'd never seen her before but I recognised her immediately. It was the halo. I'd seen it a few times since that initial experience with the nurse when I'd had my first episode, but this was different. All the others had been silvery. This woman's halo – or nimbus, aura, whatever you care to call it – was iridescent, a brilliant, rippling rainbow. And there was one other difference. This time I'd seen it without falling unconscious to the floor or going into a trance. This, I knew with complete certainty, was the Rainbow Angel.

I stared at her, unable to help myself. She was attractive, though not especially beautiful as I would have expected an angel to be. Her hair was fair, hanging down below her shoulders – not radiant and golden but still blonde enough for the part. She didn't have any wings but that wasn't a problem. She had the rainbow and that was what mattered.

She ordered tea, with a coffee for her friend, who I barely registered except when she interacted with the Rainbow Angel. They chatted, sometimes quietly then breaking into loud peals of laughter. I wasn't listening to their conversation. I was just watching, marvelling at the shimmering veil of colours that enveloped her. They had another drink, then cakes. The Rainbow Angel lit a cigarette, John Player Special from a dark blue flip-top pack.

When her friend got up to visit the café's lavatory, I stood too. I crossed the floor to where she sat and stood by her chair. For a moment I was tongue-tied, too excited and afraid to organise my thoughts into coherent speech. She became aware of my presence and looked up me, frowning as she tried to place me. When I continued to hover there saying nothing, her curiosity turned to concern.

'Is there something I can do for you? Do I know you? Are you alright?'

Her talking directly to me broke the spell. My brain

began to work again and my tongue was unlocked.

'Do you know the lost story?'

'What? What are you on about? What lost story?'

'I don't know,' I admitted. 'All I know is that you know about it. Without it my life's worthless. Please tell me.'

She seemed alarmed. Around her the rainbow stirred and darkened. 'I don't know who you are or what you're talking about. Piss off, you nutter. Piss off or I'll have the Old Bill on you.'

I was shocked. What kind of talk was this? Angels shouldn't swear, surely? As I was reeling from this development her friend returned.

'What's up, Karen – is this geezer bothering you?'

'Yeah – I told him to piss off but he's still here.'

'No,' I said, pleadingly. 'You don't understand. I only want to know about the lost story, *l'histoire perdue*. You must tell me.'

'Oi you,' the other woman shouted. 'Stop bothering my friend. She told you to piss off, so go on – piss off.'

I went away, but not quite how they expected.

I was lying on a floor somewhere. I could smell toast and bacon, coffee and fried eggs. All I could see was two pairs of legs in blue serge trousers. I could hear a woman's voice.

'...and the next thing, he just falls flat on his back in the middle of the bloody place. None of us laid a finger on him. He just fell over, like he'd been smacked in the face.'

'You said he was talking before he collapsed,' said one of the policemen. 'What did he say?'

'Kept asking me about some story he'd lost. I reckon

he's a nutter. It's his bloody marbles he's lost, not a story. He should be locked up for his own bloody good. Too many of his sort walking the streets and frightening people minding their own business.'

'Yes, miss. I know what you mean. We'll wait here until the ambulance arrives and make sure they know he might be dangerous. He's not hurt so I reckon they'll take him straight to the loony bin.'

Loony bin? The policeman thought I was mad. I had to tell him the truth. My parents had always told me never to lie to the police, and whatever the Rainbow Angel and her friend had told them I had to put it right. 'Ask the angel about the lost story,' I told them. 'I need to know what it is.' It came out in French. *Demandez à l'ange de vous enseigner sur l'histoire perdue. J'ai besoin de savoir ce que c'est.*

'Did you hear that, Sarge? I think he might be a foreigner.'

'A foreigner? No, George. I think he just called us something nasty. Cheeky bastard. Using offensive language likely to cause a breach of the peace. And resisting arrest.'

'Resisting arrest – yeah, that's right,' George agreed. 'We'll have to restrain him.'

The first kick took me in the ribs and the second struck me in the abdomen. They hauled me upright and punched me a few times, taking care not to mark my face. I heard the women laughing as the policemen beat me up. Somehow that was more terrifying than the punches and kicks.

'You're nicked, you slag. Cuff him, George.'

It was the 1970s. Everybody watched *The Sweeney*, even coppers.

I spent a month in prison, pending psychiatric tests, for the imaginary offences that had earned me a beating, plus an equally fictitious charge of assaulting a police officer. It was unpleasant, so bad that I really do not want to talk about it. Doing my time didn't earn my release, though. The next six months of my life were passed in a psychiatric ward, where I was fed drugs even more damaging than the carbamazepine and subjected to electro-convulsive therapy. That's something else I don't want to talk about.

When I was eventually pronounced cured of the psychosis I'd never had and released back into the community that didn't want me, I was a lethargic, timorous wreck, barely able to function unless given specific instructions. Inevitably, I was prescribed more drugs. At home I wouldn't even take a leak without first asking my parents' permission. I was unable to hold anything like a normal conversation, even with my mum and dad. The television upset me and radio programmes made me anxious. For a long time I couldn't even leave the house because the sky was so big it frightened me and traffic noises sent me into a panic. Nearly thirty years old, I started wetting the bed. Yes, I was clearly cured.

The wonder of it is that the ecstatic episodes continued throughout my incarceration. No matter what drugs I was given, no matter how many times electricity was shot through my brain, no matter how many invented childhood traumas I confessed to the therapists to satisfy their need to prove their own hypotheses, the episodes kept happening. I started seeing more halos without having episodes. In the hospital I saw another Rainbow Angel, a black woman who wept and wailed constantly. This time I kept my mouth shut. I did the same a few weeks after my release, when one came to our door to ask if we had heard the good news in the Bible and opened our hearts to Jesus. That didn't fool me at all. Whenever I opened my heart all that came in was darkness; and I had learned through bitter experience that the rainbow did not make the angel.

Years went by, decades. I continued to collect medication from the pharmacist once a month, to keep the doctors happy. But after the first couple of years I never took the tablets. As long as I kept out of trouble no one checked up on me. My mother died, followed a few years later by my father. The council rehoused me, putting me into this cramped flat where nothing much works. I feel quite at home here, because I don't work either. I never really recovered from prison and the psychiatric unit, though I still have my episodes and still sometimes wake from them speaking that language I never learned. Now and again I see women arrayed in shifting clouds of dazzling colours. I never approach them, never speak to them. In fact, I always look away immediately and walk in the opposite direction. I don't want any trouble. I do as I'm told and never argue with authority. I keep myself to myself, just as I've kept my nose clean all these years. I don't want people to think I really am mentally ill. I never want to go back to that hospital. I don't want to take any more of those soul-rotting drugs.

One of those women might have been the Rainbow Angel but I'm sure now that I shall never know. I accept that, just as I accept that I shall never know why I have my episodes, or why I sometimes speak in French as I'm recovering. I may never learn why I first became fixated on *l'histoire perdue* – but I think now I understand what it means.

A few months ago I bought my computer, a laptop. It was cheap but I still had to tighten my belt while I saved for it. The technology was surprisingly easy to master, though I struggled with the word-processing software and the machine is unreliable. But I had time and persistence, and quiet. I began to write, slowly and painstakingly, with many false starts. If I'd been doing it the old-fashioned way there would have been a lot of crossings-out and torn-up sheets of paper. It's hard work. It doesn't come easily to me and I labour over every paragraph, agonising over the choice of words, the length of a sentence, where to place a comma.

I'm still not sure why I began but it occurred to me that *l'histoire perdue* is really the story of what my life would have been if those episodes had never begun – if it hadn't been destroyed first by the medication then what happened when I thought I had found the Rainbow Angel at last. I cannot write *l'histoire perdue* because that lost life would be fiction, and I have proved to myself that I have no talent for that. No, this is another story, a real one. And although it is not the tale I would have liked to tell, I do not want this one too to be lost.

Asking

She asks him what he means. He shrugs and moodily kicks a pebble. Because he is leaning back on the bench and unable to get decent leverage, the kick lacks both direction and force. The pebble lazily meanders a couple of feet then rolls back down the slight gradient, coming to rest against the booted foot that had struck it. It is exactly the same colour as the boot, brown and shiny, polished by millennia.

'What I *mean*,' he says, with exaggerated patience, 'is that this conversation is going nowhere. Just like you. You know you'll never leave me. You're too afraid.'

He takes a pack of cigarettes from his coat pocket, extracts one and lights it with a match. For the thousandth time she wishes she hadn't given up smoking. Somewhere in her bag is a packet of Polo mints but she can't be bothered to rummage through all that stuff. He notices her tension and offers her a smoke, laughing when she shakes her head. He knew she wouldn't take it. He would never have offered otherwise.

'I'm not afraid of you,' she lies. Of course she's afraid – a small woman has a lot to fear from a big man notoriously handy with his fists and feet, and who has a very bad temper. She has a few fading bruises to prove it. At least she's not one of the delusional ones, the women who brainwash themselves into believing that those explosions of violence are an expression of love. She knows damned well that he doesn't love her. But he does think he owns her, and he believes that a man has the right to do whatever he wants with his property.

'If you're not afraid then go on, stand up and walk away right now. I won't try to stop you. I won't come after you.'

Now it's he who is lying.

She looks around her. There are people in the park – women with small children feeding squirrels with stale cake and peanuts, older kids playing football, dog-walkers and joggers. He wouldn't do anything with them around. He has no shame at what he does to her but he wouldn't want witnesses. It is so tempting. Stand up, walk away and never look back. But later, when there was no one looking, he would be there. He would make her pay for that humiliation seen by none.

The smouldering cigarette butt is on the ground. The nut-brown boot stamps down and extinguishes it. He leans back against the bench, completely relaxed, confident that his property will not stray. She looks at him. He's good-looking, plausible and utterly without sincerity. Ownership is all that matters to him. He can do as he pleases. She knows he has other women. He often tells her about them, smiling as he describes what they do, what they are like. He's always on the look-out for fresh meat, as he calls his conquests. That's how he sees them – territory to possess. He's particularly drawn to women with husbands or boyfriends. Trespass on other men's property excites him, makes him think he's better than those other guys. But she's his property and she must neither look nor be looked at. He's beaten men unconscious for imaginary indications of interest. He's beaten her bloody for less than that.

She does look, of course. In fact, she does more than that. She dreams.

She's dreaming now.

He lights another cigarette and once again she feels the phantom pangs of withdrawal. But she's no longer thinking about the man sitting a couple of feet from her on that park bench. She's thinking about someone from long ago, when she was young. He was a sweet boy, but she thought he was too unworldly. He hadn't known what he wanted to do with his life and was content to wait and see what happened. She'd wanted security and domestic comfort – needs instilled in her by her mother and her peers, by the time and place into which she had been born. A dreamer with no ambition or interest in material attainment was not what she wanted, no matter how much she cared about him. Love was not enough for the future she envisaged. Instead, she had got what she asked for and the taste was bitter indeed.

'Why did you do it?' she asks. The reverie is ended and she is suddenly curious.

He laughs, and it is a brief, harsh sound. 'I wanted to see if I could trust you,' he says, a sneer in his voice. 'Obviously I can't. I'll just have to keep a closer eye on you, won't I? A man has to look after what's his. Who is he, anyway?'

One solitary phone call, that was all it had been. A strained five minutes of conversation just to say hello, just to see if anything still remained. The voice at the other end of the line had been surprised, polite and reserved, but not friendly. Nothing remained there for her – another disappointment to add to the growing list. But he had found out. She hadn't known how closely he scrutinised the telephone bills, the extent to which he monitored her life. She raises her head and stares directly into the eyes of the man sitting next to her. His eyes are cold and disdainful. She is his property, nothing more. Suddenly her spirits are lifted by that dispassionate gaze. There's nothing for her there, either.

She can do this. But she has to know what he knows, to find out how far he has gone.

'What makes you think it's a man?'

This time his laugh is a snarl, a warning not to be clever. The anger is always there but now it's edging closer to the surface. 'I called the number, stupid. A bloke answered. I said I was doing a survey, asked to speak to the lady of the house. He said he didn't have a partner. Come on, don't fuck with me. Who is he?'

Her stomach feels like a small boat on a heavy sea, bobbing and spinning. She has to play this so carefully. There's no point in more lies. All she can do is tell him the truth and hope he chokes on it.

'It was someone I used to know, an old boyfriend. I thought it would be nice to call him. I hadn't spoken to him in years. He's doing well for himself. It was good to catch up.'

'An old boyfriend, eh? What, were you hoping to hook up with him again?'

The question terminates on a sneering note that is

both a put-down and a dare. She sighs and stands, stretching her arms that somehow seem to need more room than they did a minute or so before. She stretches them like a bird extending its wings. Behind her, the sun stabs bright rays through a gap in the clouds. He has been looking up at her but now he flinches and looks away as the light hurts his eyes.

'Yes,' she tells him, her arms still outstretched. 'I was, actually. He was a nice guy when I knew him and he still is. He told me straight that he didn't want to see me; that he had moved on a long time ago. He's a successful artist now. I thought something might happen but now I know it won't. And you know what? It's a relief. After I called him I realised that it wasn't what I wanted at all.'

He grins, secure in the knowledge that his triumph is complete. 'There you are, then,' he tells her. 'I said you'd never leave me and I was right. But don't you ever lie to me again, you hear? Otherwise you'll really be asking for trouble.'

Now it's she who is smiling. Her extended arms seem so long and light and strong, like vast sails of feather and bone. The sunlight behind her is now very bright. He squints up at her. She realises that he is by no means as confident as he is trying to sound.

'No more lies,' she agrees. 'I don't want him and I don't want you, either. I don't want you or anything of yours. I don't want you controlling me all the time. I don't want to live in fear of you and your fists anymore. I don't want to be another possession in the inventory of your life. Ten years of you has been more than enough. What I want is to be my own woman. I've never been that before.'

She turns and walks away, into the sun. As she closes her eyes against the beautiful glare she hears him standing and taking the first angry step after her. But she does not quicken her pace or even consider running from him. Whatever he does now, she doesn't belong to him. She has gone.

Shots

Suddenly, a shot rang out. Everyone in the bar turned to look at me, startled by the unexpectedly loud sound. I don't know why I'd slammed the glass down so hard on the table. Maybe it was because this bar was so pretentiously modern and I'd unconsciously chosen to make a protest. Glass tables do not belong in bars. Drunks and glass structures larger than a glass or bottle generally do not mix well. Hadn't these people heard of health and safety?

I was mildly surprised that the table was still in one piece. The only discernible damage was the burning sensation in my throat as the tequila attempted a quick getaway. I was a little surprised by that. The previous six had stayed down without making a fuss. Maybe that last one hadn't wanted company. It would just have to get used to crowds.

Standing was an interesting experience. Waiting to be served at the bar was less entertaining. By the time I was in the barman's sights my seat had been taken by a young woman whose empty-headed loudness was matched only by the shortness of her skirt, surrounded by slightly older men who all thought they were in with a chance. I didn't care about any of that but I did mind when the barman said 'I'm sorry sir, I think you've had enough. I'll have to ask you to leave.'

I didn't make a fuss, merely smiled and nodded as I put the twenty-pound note I'd been waving back in my pocket. I don't like to be unwelcome anywhere, and you never know when you'll need a bar in a hurry. I wove unsteadily through the crowd of fellow drinkers – I hadn't noticed any of them entering – and left for another boozer.

The Bunch of Grapes had changed since I had last been there. It had been years, I realised. Now the clientele were mainly young professionals of an even trendier persuasion that those in the previous establishment. I must have been twenty years older than the oldest of them, and the least expensively dressed. I was also the only person there who didn't have a smartphone surgically attached. I wasn't going to hang around for long. I ordered a pint of Becks and a tequila shot. This time I placed the glass gently on the table when I had poured it down my neck. I didn't bother with more than a couple of mouthfuls of the lager. It was flat and tasted slightly sour. My hangover was going to be bad enough without inviting trouble.

The George, an old coaching inn dating back to the Middle Ages, was even more crowded. There was no room inside, only a throbbing mass of people between me and the bar. I decided to give it a miss. It was, after all, only a short stroll to the Blue Eyed Maid and it was still early. But that pub too had changed for the worse. It had become a 'sports bar' and was thronged with young men shouting at a television screen showing a Champions League match between Chelsea and a team from somewhere in Eastern

Europe. At least the football was distracting the punters and allowed me a free run to the bar so I could fortify myself for the next sortie. Two large vodkas later, I was back on the street, *en route* to a quiet little pub I knew in the backstreets to the west of Borough High Street.

And this one was quiet. Apart from me there were only two old boys discussing politics, a young couple who spent the entire time I was there not talking to each other, and a bored woman of about my own age working behind the bar. I settled down and proceeded to drink seriously.

This was a proper pub, one that welcomed the drinker. Like backstreet pubs everywhere this one recognised that it made its money by selling drinks to people who drank them. There would be none of that 'I'm sorry sir, I think you've had enough' in this bar, not unless I went crazy and started tearing the place apart. No, they knew that the solitary drinker had only one aim: to drink, and in drinking, to forget. I was all for forgetting. That was indeed why I was drinking.

To be honest, I could have done it in my flat. A bottle of vodka and a few beers from the supermarket would have cost only a fraction of what I'd already spent, and I wouldn't have had to worry about getting home. But if there's something a bit sad about a middle-aged man drinking alone in a pub, the same man doing it in domestic isolation is simply tragic. I was depressed but I wasn't that far bloody gone. I could still at least affect the pretence of social drinking. I bought two tequilas and a pint of Stella. Then I had the same again.

The first inkling I had that something was wrong was the

ringing of the alarm clock. I never set mine and in any case it makes a beeping noise. I only know that because I once accidentally had the alarm switched on while attempting to put the clock right when the battery had gone flat.

The second clue was the warm body I could feel next to mine. I live on my own and am seemingly permanently between girlfriends. I don't have a cat or dog either. Company in bed is something that rarely happens to me. It had been a very long time since I heard anyone but me snoring.

Conclusive evidence came with the sight that greeted me when I opened my eyes. I was in a bed that wasn't mine, in a room I didn't recognise. And I was in bed with a woman I didn't remember meeting. All things considered, it could have been worse. At least I'd woken up next to a woman. Or so I hoped. I gently lifted the duvet and checked. The top half of my bedmate looked wholly female, which was a relief. I was briefly tempted to make a closer inspection but that might have been more trouble than it was worth.

I closed my eyes again, partly because I still harboured a faint hope that this might all be a dream and I would find myself safely in my own bed when I opened them again; but mostly because the hangover was really, really bad. Every part of my body hurt but thankfully the daylight's painful assault on my retinas was easily sorted by lowering my eyelids. The rest was probably going to take a while. I hoped the woman, whoever she was, had a good supply of painkillers.

When I was fairly sure I could stand that brilliant glare – actually it was a dull, grey and overcast morning, but you know how it is – I opened my eyes a fraction and gingerly got up. Well, it was that or pissing the bed. The woman stirred, muttered something I couldn't quite make out, then settled back to sleep. I had a quick look but couldn't see my boxer shorts anywhere. In fact, I couldn't see any of the strewn clothing one normally associates with a night of impromptu passion. Perhaps we'd got started in another room? Which begged the questions – just how passionate had the night been and why couldn't I remember any of it? The second part was obviously connected with the reason I didn't recognise the woman, or remember anything after my fifth – or perhaps seventh – tequila shot in that last pub, assuming it had been the last boozer I'd visited. I shelved the questions. I had no answers to either of them and I desperately needed a slash. Hopefully the toilet wouldn't be too hard to find.

Just as I was opening the bedroom door the woman sleepily called out. 'George? Put the kettle on, love.'

My name, which I will not divulge in case anyone I know is reading this memoir, is not George. I quietly closed the door, located the bathroom and took a leak, then retrieved my clothing and dressed as quickly and quietly as I could. The front door made a loud noise as I shut it behind me but by then I was away on my toes. I'd only gone out for a couple of bloody drinks and my life was complicated enough.

I was just exiting the street door at the bottom of a deep stairwell when a bloke barged past me. He was big and steroid-bulky, with close-cropped iron-grey hair, cauliflower ears and a nose that looked as if it had been broken more than once; a seriously nasty-looking and very pissed-off geezer. He swore at me, even though I had been trying to stand aside when he crashed into me. I merely apologised and tried to look contrite when he glared at me with hard piggy eyes and hauled his muscle-bound body up the stairs. Around his neck there was one of those chunky gold necklaces with a name in big blingy letters: GEORGE.

That had been a really fucking close shave.

I hadn't a clue where I was but after wandering around for half an hour or so I found myself outside Pimlico tube station. I live in Brixton and had been drinking in the Borough, the familiar hostelries close to where I work. God knows how I'd ended up in Pimlico. I bought a bottle of sparkling mineral water at a newsagent and drank half of it in one go. It had been a funny old evening, I reflected. I'd gone out for a quiet pint and a bit of non-contact company after coming home from work to find a message on my answerphone informing me that one of my oldest friends had died. He was an old drinking pal and we'd been in plenty of drunken scrapes together so it seemed appropriate to go out and raise a glass or two in his memory at a couple of our old haunts. I honestly hadn't intended to get totally hammered but the sense of my own mortality had filled me with a deep gloom that simply had to be addressed. After that I suppose I'd just been caught up in the moment.

The woman bothered me. She was very attractive and looked around ten years older than me, which would put her in her late fifties. Mind you, on a morning after a night before I usually look a decade older than I really am. I have no problem with age-difference. Why, I have often tried to pull women much younger than myself. Nothing ventured, nothing gained, as they say. Nothing gained, certainly. My attempts have spanned the full range of success, from utter failure to abject humiliation. It was nice to have actually had some luck, even if the woman was somewhat senior to the women I normally drunkenly propositioned. Our respective ages were immaterial. There was nothing wrong with two consenting adults enjoying a night of mutual pleasure, even if one half of them couldn't remember a damned thing about it and the other one had mistaken him for someone else. No, I told myself, no harm had been done and a good time had hopefully been had by all.

With a clear conscience and a wistful reproach to my drunken amnesia, I went into the tube station and fished the Oyster card from my wallet. And that's when I found that my business cards were missing. Yes, my business cards. Small white cardboard rectangles with my name, work extension and mobile phone number, and the address of my workplace printed in indigo and bloody well *embossed*. No expense spared at Tallifer and Sons Security Limited, unless you counted the pay.

I felt as pale as I must have looked. I had surely left them at that woman's flat – that woman I had spent the night with. That woman who had called out in her sleep to a man named George; a man who must have been the brute heading towards her flat as I was going in the other direction and who seemed to have taken an instant dislike to me. Cursing my drunkenness and stupidity I bolted into the tube station and made my trembling way home to Brixton.

Tallifer and Sons sells locks, dead-bolts, reinforced doors, metal grilles and bars (not that kind) to the fearful and security-conscious citizens of South London. We also have a nice range of CCTV, burglar alarms, personal alarms and motion sensors. For a few quid we can also quietly provide pepper sprays, Mace and stuff even less legal, no questions asked. Percy Tallifer, the head honcho, unaffectionately known as the Old Bastard to all the staff (excluding his oily sons, Walter and Gibson, a pair of sneaky, treacherous, venal arseholes for whom no nickname could be sufficiently obscene) had once even sourced a sawn-off shotgun and a couple of dozen cartridges for a turf accountant who had refused to pay the local youth posse for the protection a shooter could provide far more cheaply and permanently. The firearm had been used. To this day I still don't know how the bloke got away with it, but he somehow convinced a jury that he had wrested the sawn-off from one of the gang members and that it had accidentally gone off six times, messily kneecapping half a dozen of South West London's most dangerous gangstas. His explanation for the five reloadings was that every time the gun had been fired it was reclaimed by one of the gang and reloaded, so he'd had to start all over again. Mysteriously, the CCTV, supplied by Tallifer and Sons, had malfunctioned for the entire twenty minutes it took for this remarkable series of events to unfold. Some juries will buy anything but I suspected that in this case it was the jury that had been bought.

But I digress. The point is that I was sorely tempted to ask the Old Bastard if he could get me a similar weapon. I reckoned it would take more than a winning smile and an apology for shagging his lady friend to stop George in his tracks. Anyway, it was beside the point. The Old Bastard had once sacked one of my colleagues for spending a night in the cells after a drunken brawl over a woman, even though she had been the woman in question and had only been arrested by mistake. While the Old Bastard was happy to make a few quid by flogging guns to select customers it was an unspoken condition of our employment that any trouble with the law would not be tolerated. Percy Tallifer had a reputation to uphold and a position of trust in the community to maintain. Sure, we all knew what sort of man he really was but as long as no one else knew it he could keep right on pretending. I had half a mind to ask one of the Sons if they would be willing to help me out but I knew they would grass me up to the Old Bastard in a heartbeat. I would just have to make my own arrangements.

As it was a Sunday, I didn't have to go to work, so I reckoned I was safe enough for the rest of the day. But it was a fair bet that George would be making a bee-line to Tallifer and Sons at a rate of knots the next morning, and he would not be a happy gorilla. I definitely had to get myself some protection. But where could I get hold of anything more persuasive than a rolled-up newspaper on a Sunday? I made coffee and leafed through the Argos catalogue. A selection of handguns or small-gauge artillery would have been useful but there was nothing resembling projectile weapons in the book. Some of the power tools looked fairly threatening, as did the gardening implements and sports equipment, but I could hardly go into work toting an angle-grinder, a rake or a set of golf clubs.

My local, the Masons Arms, usually featured a few iffy-looking characters who would probably be able to lay their hands on anything from weed and prostitutes to nerve gas and nuclear missiles, but they were the sort of men who never spoke to anyone outside their own circle, unless it was to tell them to fuck off and die, not necessarily in that order. There was no way I was asking them. They probably had mates who made George look like a flower-arranger.

My own friends wouldn't be much help. They were mainly office-workers. I work in the office at Tallifer and Sons but I also go out to advise people on domestic security, measure up and give estimates. That makes me the hardest of my circle of friends by a very long way.

I didn't sleep much that night. Whenever I shut my eyes all I could see was George's ugly mug, twisting into a cruel little grin whenever he removed another part of my anatomy. By the time Monday morning dawned, I was terrified.

Although sorely tempted to call in sick, I turned up for work as usual. I'd managed to convince myself that the alarm we had connected to the local police station – the Old Bastard was as terrified of being robbed of a single penny as I was of being beaten to a bloody pulp by George – would have the boys in blue round at the double if danger threatened. Even so I was not my usual chirpy self. 'Cheer up, mate,' said one customer. 'It might never happen.' Yes, I thought glumly, but it probably will. George hadn't looked the kind of guy to pass over someone even *thinking* about him the wrong way. And I'd had sex with his girlfriend, probably. I was, as they say, bricking it.

But the day passed without incident. I kept my wits about me on the way home, to make sure I wasn't being followed by something nasty, brutish and anything but short, but everything appeared to be kosher. The next day was much the same, and the day after that. By Friday afternoon I was starting to think I was in the clear. Perhaps I hadn't left my business cards at the woman's flat after all – maybe I'd simply lost them while I was wandering around London as drunk as a skunk. Or she might have found them and disposed of them before George arrived. Yes, I'd been worrying myself sick over nothing. For the first time since that Sunday morning, I began to relax.

Inevitably, that was exactly when George stalked through the door of Tallifer and Sons. He was with another bloke cut from the same cloth, possibly his uglier brother. They were both carrying sawn-off shotguns and looked well up for a spot of summary retribution.

Naturally, that happened when I was on my own, minding the shop while the others were out on business – except for the Sons, who were on their semi-permanent lunch-break – and I was on the opposite side of the showroom from the alarm, so I couldn't even call for help. I was royally screwed. For a moment the contents of my guts threatened to acquaint themselves with the inside of my boxer shorts, but I controlled myself. If I was going to suffer or die it would be with a modicum of dignity, though bravery was wholly out of the question.

'You,' George snarled, pointing the sawn-off in my direction. 'You know what I fucking want. Don't do anything fucking silly, you hear me?'

Don't do anything silly? I'd already done the silly thing and now I was going to pay well over the odds for it. I nodded mutely.

George squinted at me. 'Here, do I fucking know you?'

Now he was playing with me. I shrugged as helplessly as I could. Then his mate, who had been watching the door, chimed in. 'Just do the fucker, George. Sooner this is over with, the fucking better, right?'

'Shame there ain't any fucking witnesses,' grinned George. 'I'm really in the mood for it today. Alright, you – get down on the fucking floor, face down. Come on, I haven't got all fucking day.'

I did as I was told. Face down suited me just fine. At least I wouldn't see it coming. I rested my left cheek against the parquet floor and closed my eyes. It would all be over with before I knew it. For the first time in nearly a week, I felt at peace. George pressed the cold, hard barrel of the shotgun against the back of my head.

Suddenly, a shot rang out.

The Ship in Borough Road, a quarter or mile or so from the shop, was crowded, as it usually was on a Friday night. I'd had a few drinks and was in the mood for quite a few more. The police had finished questioning me and told me I was free to go, though I was told I'd have to go to the police station at some point to make a statement. I suppose I should have been in shock but I was so thankful to still be alive and kicking that it hadn't crossed my mind to react in any way other than sheer bloody delighted gratitude.

I'd stuck with religious fervour to the Old Bastard's story. George and his mate had burst into the shop with two sawn-off shotguns and a handgun. When they'd threatened to blow my legs off if I didn't open the safe, I'd agreed to do as they demanded. Just then Mr Tallifer had come out of the back room to see what was happening.

While the two armed robbers were distracted I had attempted to wrest the handgun from George and it had gone off, twice. By a fluke both intruders had been shot in the head, killing them instantly, and saving my life and the Old Bastard's. Mysteriously, the CCTV had malfunctioned for the entire ten minutes of my ordeal. Tallifer had expressed his disappointment to the Chief Inspector in charge of the police response team. He would be terminating his contract with that supplier immediately. Tallifer and Sons would not sell shoddy goods to their valued clients, he announced. The police seemed impressed.

George, it turned out, had a fair bit of form. Armed robbery, GBH, threatening behaviour – you name it, if it involved visiting physical violence on others, he'd either done it or was in the frame. I supposed he'd decided to mix business with pleasure, relieving Tallifer and Sons of a week's profit and taking me out at the same time. His accomplice wasn't far behind in the mayhem and bodily damage stakes. The Old Bill reckoned I'd been lucky. The Old Bastard reckoned the hours he'd put in on the firing range had been well worth it, though if I ever repeated that to anyone I would be out of a job and sued for slander. I reckoned I would make a point of never crossing the Old Bastard in any way whatsoever. The mess had been horrible.

Now I was celebrating my continued existence with my colleagues and – every silver lining has a cloud – the Sons, neither of whom had yet put his hand in his pocket for a round of drinks. The Old Bastard had declined to join us, claiming tiredness. I figured he'd probably gone home to watch the allegedly non-existent recording of himself blowing away two of South London's most notorious villains. It was OK, though. I was getting nicely pissed and was definitely pleased that I was still alive to do so.

It was my round. Inevitably none of my colleagues could be bothered to get off their arses to help me with the drinks, so I went to the bar on my own. When I eventually reached the hallowed wooden altar, I had a shock. Standing between me and a round of drinks was the woman I had spent the night with the previous Saturday, with a woman who looked like her much younger sister. They were drinking something with Coke or Pepsi. I asked her to excuse me so I could get to the bar. She smiled at me as I squeezed into the small space she made for me.

'You look familiar,' she said. 'Have we met?'

'I'm sure I would remember if we'd met when I was sober,' I gallantly replied. 'But I might not if I'd been drinking. Maybe if you told me your name it might jog my memory.'

You never know your luck. After all, I'd got lucky six days earlier, probably. And that Friday night I felt very lucky indeed.

'I'm Gloria,' she said, a definite flirtatious sparkle in her eye. 'This is my daughter Georgina, but we all call her George. She stays with me sometimes, don't you George?'

'Not lately, though,' said George. 'My boyfriend's home on leave from Afghanistan, so I'll be in my own bed again tonight.'

'Ladies,' I said. 'My name's Craig.' It isn't, of course – but I told them my real name, the one you won't hear. 'Tonight I'm celebrating having survived an armed robbery. It'll be in the papers tomorrow, I expect. Please allow me to buy you both a drink. What would you like?'

'That's very nice of you,' Gloria responded, pressing herself against me as the crowd at the bar thickened. 'I don't know what to have, though. I'm fed up with Bacardi and Coke, it's a bit sickly after the first couple, isn't it George? What do you suggest, Craig?'

I didn't think about it for long. 'How do you girls fancy a couple of tequila shots?'

Milestone

A leaden grey sky and a cold, driving wind that makes him shiver, even though it is outside and he can't really feel it biting at his skin from the shelter of his bedroom. But he'll be out in it soon and can anticipate the chill. He doesn't like winter even though it brings Christmas and his birthday. Cakes and presents do not compensate for the short, gloomy days and dull skies that make him feel sad and somehow much lonelier than he really is; and he is a solitary boy, ill at ease in company and prone to moments of helpless fear when boredom leaves him with too much to think about. He gets bored often, when there's nothing entertaining on television and he's run out of books and comics to read, and the notepaper has been used up so he is unable to draw or write the stories that rise up from some unfathomable place deep in his mind. There are no more toys, not at his age, and he has yet to learn what will replace them. The empty times are vacuums that must be filled, and the demons of anxiety require no second invitation. School is worse, a narrow path with taunts and violence on one side, and fearful tedium on the other, as he is forced to participate in lessons on subjects he cannot quite grasp and his frequent failures bring punishment and humiliation. The time between waking and arrival at the school gate is a nightmare of apprehension; the ensuing ordeal is almost a relief.

At least this morning has brought a puzzle, something to pique his interest. From his bedroom window he can see that someone has deposited a loose, untidy bundle of rags and other rubbish in the middle of the road, a couple of hundred yards away from his home. It distracts him, slowing his reluctant preparations for the school day ahead. Indeed, the sight transfixes him. It's a strange and inconvenient place to dump anything. He's surprised that no one has yet stopped their car, annoyed at the obstruction, and got out to curse and move it to one side. But then he has yet to see either vehicles or pedestrians, and on such a quiet street motorists would simply have driven round it to save precious seconds on their way to work. It's a cold, gloomy morning and rain is in the air, promised by those clouds. Who would want to be out among the elements on such a day if they didn't absolutely have to?

The thought makes him sadder still. He wants to stay at home, warm in his bed, tucked up with a book and perhaps a mug of hot chocolate. He sighs and half-heartedly shrugs into his blue school blazer, but continues to look at the rubbish in the road. It vaguely reminds him of something but he is unable to identify what that might be. Then he sees Mrs Shreeves the lollipop lady walking up the street toward his house, in her big white coat with a fluorescent orange band and carrying her lollipop sign that says *STOP* and *CHILDREN CROSSING* in bold black letters on a white background inside a red circle. Today she has a transparent plastic hood over the peaked cap that never quite restrains her curly brown hair and is wearing Wellington boots.

The boy likes Mrs Shreeves, who is always cheerful and friendly whatever the weather and who he thinks has the kindest face he's ever seen. He's too old now to really need to use the school crossing, and it's a little out of his way, but he always takes a slightly longer route to school just so he can see her and say hello, and receive one of her smiles in return. She's old – at least thirty – and isn't very pretty, not by a twelve year old boy's standards, but she is nice. One day he will look back and realise that the kindness radiating from within her makes her not merely pretty but extraordinarily beautiful, and that her twinkle-eyed, slightly lop-sided smile is actually quite sexy; but that is a long way off in the future, when the hormones already at work in his body turn him into a young man. For now he is content to acknowledge that he will see at least one friendly face on his way to the daily torment that is secondary education.

As he watches, Mrs Shreeves stops suddenly and puts a gloved hand to her mouth. Then she drops the lollipop to the pavement and, awkward in those boots and the bulk of her coat, runs into the middle of the road, where she kneels down by the bundle of rubbish. She reaches down and begins to turn the pile over in a flutter of heavy black and blue cloth and bent sticks. Small objects spill from a blue bag that is detached from the heap as it is moved. A small shiny item rolls across the road and comes to rest against the kerb.

He freezes, all thoughts of school draining from his head as if someone has pulled out a plug. His vision somehow becomes telescopic, zooming in so that details he shouldn't be able to make out are clearly visible. Later he won't be quite sure what he has really observed and what his fertile imagination has conjured up to fill the gaps – or if there would be any difference between the two. Mrs Shreeves is now pushing at part of the pile, massaging it, dipping her head every now and then to press her face against the white ovoid that had been revealed when the pile was turned over. A man and woman come rushing out of their house to join her, wearing coats but still in carpet-slippers. Then other people appear as if from nowhere, until there is a small crowd gathered round that forlorn object lying in the road. A black car pulls up and the driver, a grey-haired man in a pin-striped suit, gets out. Mrs Shreeves looks up at the figures surrounding her and shakes her head. Then she too stands. It is the first time he has ever seen her upset about anything. Now the pile of rubbish has rearranged to reveal two thin, pale projections terminating in white canvas shoes wholly inadequate for the weather. Mrs Shreeves' shoulders start to shake and she puts her hands over her face.

The boy finally understands the true nature of the scene he has watched unfolding and the revelation is too much for him. He turns away from the window at last and he too covers his face with his hands as he begins to weep for his first encounter with death. This, he knows, is a milestone, the first of many deaths he will meet on that road leading to an unknown point in the future, when it would be his turn. And if he feels this unexpected grief at the death of a complete stranger, how will he feel when he loses people he loves? How could he possibly deal with that?

All at once, school is a less worrying prospect than it had been only a few minutes ago. His fear of the teachers and playground thugs, algebra and French, has diminished in the face of the losses to come. It is no comfort, none at all. The light in his bedroom dims as the clouds darken, and raindrops are spat noisily against the window with the wind's rising fury. The boy sniffs, wipes away his tears with a blue sleeve and steals one last look at the silent, respectful people surrounding the dead woman lying in the road in the rain. The crowd has thinned by one. Mrs Shreeves has left them and is walking up the road on her way to the school crossing, her lollipop retrieved. As she nears his house, she suddenly looks up at his bedroom window, sees him staring gravely down at her, and smiles sadly, her face wet with tears or rain, he cannot tell which. For once her eyes do not sparkle – and in a way, that is the very worst of what he has witnessed. In a surprisingly grown-up moment he wishes he could hold her and tell her everything will be alright. He wants to kiss away those tears and bring the light back to her smile. A little shocked and ashamed of himself for these mildly inappropriate thoughts, he weakly returns the smile and tries to wave to her. But he cannot raise his hand, which has become as heavy as his heart.

Copy Error #47

The fingers weren't right. They were long enough, the correct shape and they all worked. Most of them were in the proper place. And there was the rub: the eight fingers and two thumbs that were exactly where they should have been were supplemented by an additional three fingers and a thumb that shouldn't have been there at all. Other than that, she was perfect. It was a shame, and he was tempted to keep her – those supernumerary digits suggested interesting erotic possibilities – but she had to go back. After the last time – the extra ear on the left side of her head that he hadn't noticed until they went to the pub – he really didn't want the neighbours talking again.

The Replication Manager was very understanding but was slightly more defensive than usual. 'I do apologise, sir. We've never had this problem before.'

'This the forty-sixth time I've had to bring her back. Don't they get inspected before they leave the workshop?'

'I'm sure it isn't the forty-sixth time, sir.'

'Well, there was the third eye, the two eyebrows on her left side, the single breast with four nipples in the middle of her chest, the one where her anus hadn't been included, the time she had two right feet, the upside-down lips, the back-to-front knees... You must have records but I've got a list somewhere, if you need one.'

'Yes, I suppose we have seen you here rather a lot. It's puzzling. She's practically the only one who hasn't come out right first time. Copy errors are so rare with TPR. We'll need to carry out a full check that she hasn't been genetically compromised.'

'You've checked that every single time and found nothing. It's just shoddy workmanship and at these prices it simply isn't good enough. Look, I'll give it one more try, OK? But if the next one fails to meet my expectations I shall demand a refund, plus compensation for the distress this has caused. It was bad enough when she originally died, but having to go through that time after time – well, it's very upsetting.'

'A refund?'

'You heard me. I've read the contract. If the cloning of my deceased wife does not result in a perfect replica, I am entitled to full reimbursement plus compensation for the trauma of her secondary demise. And I should point out that it's gone well past the secondary stage. I'll come back a week from today and you can euthanise this one and I'll collect the replacement. And this time I want to inspect her thoroughly before I take her home. If I'm dissatisfied again you'd better have your chequebook handy.'

Life was cheap in 2043. The wealthy and powerful were worth quite a bit, but you couldn't give the poor away. You couldn't get them back, either – the cost of Total Person Replication was beyond the pockets of all but the select few, the movers and shakers who controlled the economy, the glitzy celebrities whose lives and lifestyles were consumed by the masses like a drug addict sucked up heroin or cocaine. The poor may not have been worth much but it was their spending that cemented the plutocracy on the topmost perch. It was simple arithmetic – if eight billion people spent a dollar each per month on cheap, mindless entertainment, it came to quite a few bucks. They also had to pay for food, accommodation, fuel and clothing. All that money went into a relative handful of bank accounts. So the poor couldn't afford TPR but they paid for the elite to be able to.

The technology was complex. It had required major breakthroughs in DNA amplification, cloning, cellular propagation, quantum computing and neurological programming. Consequently, the cost was huge. The first TPR was carried out at the behest of a Russian oligarch fixated on mid-twentieth-century Hollywood stars. Monroe had been followed by Bogart and Bacall, Burton and Taylor. Now the world was crawling with resurrected idols – there were at least three replicas of Elvis, two Michael Jacksons and six or seven Winston Churchills, which was a bit of a surprise to everyone when the news came out, though it certainly cheered up UKIP and the Tories. One luxury mansion on the outskirts of Moscow allegedly boasted a Khrushchev and a JFK, who reportedly spent their days arguing, when Nikita wasn't too drunk to stand and Jack wasn't busy bedding the maids. A Saudi prince was rumoured to have a Princess Di. In LA a supergroup comprising Jimi Hendrix, Keith Moon, Jim Morrison and Sid Vicious played a perpetual residency at Caesar's Palace, much to the delight of various West Coast drug dealers and liquor stores. As yet there had been no move to bring back Kurt Cobain – everyone had a good idea where that would lead. In London the Houses of Parliament had a room set aside for former prime ministers who really should have remained six feet under – and one in particular who many current MPs wished was back below ground for good. Mrs T was never as popular as she still liked to believe.

With the new technology, TPR was easy. All you needed were a few cells – a tooth, some hairs, a shard of bone or a tissue sample, even a smear of dried saliva on an old envelope – biographical materials, video footage, a hairstylist and wardrobe consultant, and an awful lot of money. Soon prices came down enough for even the second-tier rich to be able to afford it. It still cost an awful lot of money, though.

Touchingly, and rather surprisingly considering the burgeoning celebrity obsession of the twenty-first century, quite a few people didn't opt for a pet film or pop star. There were those who wanted nothing more than to be reunited with a loved one who had been taken from them in tragic circumstances. A much-mourned son or daughter, a beloved husband or wife – that was all some people wanted. It gave the public a warm glow. Ultra-conservative politicians and clerics couldn't exactly rail against the resurrection of loved ones – not when the people were so firmly for it. And certainly not when the Vatican had several deceased popes and a handful of saints wandering through its corridors, and when the late Osama Bin Laden was being troublesome in the Middles East again. Religions, like governments, were usually happy to change their tune if it would gain them an advantage.

Of course, the poor demanded access to the new technology. And they could keep on demanding because it wasn't going to happen. It was a nice idea but in the first place none of them could afford it, and in the second place a world with nearly nine billion people swarming across its surface could hardly countenance what was in effect immortality – and even multiplicity – for all, especially the poor.

So life was cheap but extended life was astonishingly expensive. That was why only people like Nick Coleridge, a highly successful property dealer, could afford to have TPR for their deceased loved ones. The technology was now tried and trusted, and rarely failed. Except in the case of Beth Coleridge, who was about to die for the forty-seventh time and would shortly be born for the forty-eighth.

'Glass of wine, dear? They've given us a nice Cabernet Sauvignon. There you go. You make yourself comfortable. I'm just popping out for a minute.'

The plexiglass door slid shut and locked itself behind him. Inside the sealed chamber Beth 47 sipped her wine, looked up at smiled at him as he looked back. It was heartbreaking. Everything was exactly as it used to be: her hair colour and style, the dimples when she smiled, the twinkle in her eyes, the way she held herself. Then she waggled her fingers affectionately. All those fingers.

Nick sighed heavily and waited for it to happen, noting how quickly and completely her face relaxed as the gas took hold. It took only a few seconds to work. He wiped away a tear as his wife died again. Poor Beth 47 – eight days of life, then out with the lights. Still, it was for the best. Winters were getting colder and it would have been a nightmare finding gloves to fit her.

In the display room, two women technicians were nervously examining the latest Beth. Nick supposed they'd been given a serious talking-to about the string of spectacular failures that were Beths 2 through to 47. He wouldn't be surprised to learn that the refund and compensation would come out of their wages. After all, it was standard practice in this day and age. Why should any sane employer accept responsibility and pay out good money when they could blame the workers and make them pay? Fortunately, governments – almost wholly drawn from the friends and relatives of the individuals who ran the corporate enterprises that bankrolled politics – agreed with that principle and it had for several years been a cornerstone of employment law in most countries.

One of the technicians saw Nick hovering outside and beckoned him to enter, clasping her hands together as he entered. The display room was decked out like the lounge of any moderately expensive hotel room. Beth 48 stood on a Persian rug, naked and unmoving save for the rise and fall of her breasts as she breathed. Her eyes were wide open but unblinking and unseeing. Nick walked around her, looking her up and down.

'Can she hear me and understand what I'm saying?'

'Oh yes, sir,' said the other technician obsequiously. 'She can obey simple commands. But that's only temporary. When the programming is activated she will think, feel and respond like any other human being, an intelligent and independent individual. Her mind and personality will be those of your wife.'

'Good.' Nick addressed Beth 48. 'Open your mouth, please.'

Beth 48 opened her mouth. Nick counted what he thought was the standard complement of incisors, canines, pre-molars and molars; one normal-looking tongue, and an unremarkable set of tonsils. He looked her over again. Two breasts with one nipple apiece; two arms and two legs; a left foot and a right foot, on the correct legs; normal numbers of toes and fingers; two buttocks; the appropriate numbers and arrangement of facial features. She looked exactly the right age.

'I take it you've given her the full survey?'

'Oh yes, sir,' the first technician replied. 'We deployed the full range of X-rays, ultrasound, MRI and CAT scans... everything. Plus a full DNA work-up. We have been most careful to ensure that no further copy errors have occurred.'

'So – she has two lungs, two kidneys, one liver, one heart, one spleen? A fully formed and functional reproductive system? Optimal motor and neural functions? A digestive tract that – um – goes all the way through?'

'Yes, sir,' said the second technician. 'We triple-checked and everything is absolutely normal. When we activate the programming, this replica will be indistinguishable from the original Beth. If you would like to take a seat we'll leave the room and you can take her for a test drive.'

'A test drive? She's not a bloody car!'

'My apologies, sir. It was just a figure of speech. Please, be seated and have a glass of complimentary champagne. Pour one for Mrs Coleridge. I expect she'll be thirsty, seeing as she's never had anything to drink before. Only one glass, mind, as she won't be used to alcohol.'

The technicians left the room. Nick poured two glasses of bubbly – it was unfair that he'd had to see off number 47 with cheap Sauvignon while welcoming number 48 with a good Bollinger. It was bad enough that the rejected versions of Beth had to die over and over, without treating them as if they didn't matter. He made a mental note to put in yet another complaint to the management. This place might be where the trendy people went for TPR but as far as Nick could see they were just a bunch of bloody cowboys. Actually, come to think of it, wasn't this the same firm that had brought back Billy the Kid and Jesse James a couple of years ago? How many people had died when they stole a couple of police horses and robbed that bank in Victoria Street? If Pat Garrett and Wyatt Earp hadn't arrived at the scene when the outlaws started shooting the hostages it would have been a complete bloodbath.

He was still ruminating about this when Beth blinked, smiled and raised the glass to her lips. 'Oh dear,' she laughed. 'I seem to have forgotten to get dressed! I think I must have had one of my turns. The last thing I can remember is watching *Panorama* with David Frost interviewing that man who claimed to have Adolf Hitler making plans for a new Thousand Year Reich in that secret bunker in Austria.'

'You just can't tell nowadays,' Nick replied. 'Everyone thought the Stalins were only a rumour until two of them appeared on that Russian chat show and beat each other to a pulp. Each claimed the other was an impostor.'

'And do you remember the two Oliver Reeds on the *New Russell Harty Show*? That was awful – they should never have let them near the hospitality room. Mind you, it was hilarious when they took all their clothes off and started wrestling. For a while there I thought Harty was going to join in.'

Nick laughed. 'Come on, dear,' he said. 'Get dressed and let's go home.'

Beth's TPR was guaranteed for three months, the industry standard set down in the Replication Trading Standards Act of 2036. It was considered a reasonable time to allow for replication flaws to become evident, and for any human being to be expected to survive without the intervention of illness, accident or foul play. It was also the optimum period for psychological acclimatisation. At the end of the three months Nick and Beth would attend a meeting with an accredited counsellor who would gently and sympathetically explain to Beth 48 that her original life had come to an end and that she had been reborn into a new body. In the meantime, Nick had to play it carefully – as far as Beth was concerned, nearly eighteen months had passed in the blink of an eye. She had to be kept away from newspapers, television, the internet, and most of the people she knew. It was a delicate and complicated business but Nick had been guided through it by the counsellor they had been assigned, a man who had himself died and been returned to the world by TPR. All he had to do was keep her distracted – and make sure she was regularly dosed with drugs designed to suppress her curiosity and independence. He'd been mildly alarmed to find out they were the same drugs used in the increasingly overcrowded prisons to keep the inmates docile but had been assured the drugs were non-addictive and had no side-effects. There would be no lasting harm. She would only be taking them for a few months, after all.

The first three months of Beth 48's life went quite well. Like all the other Beths, the drugs made her a bit dreamy and sometimes forgetful, and she was easily confused by all the little changes Nick had made since her initial death – the kitchen scissors now resided in a different drawer, there was a new coffee-maker, and the books and Blu-rays had all been rearranged. Those things were easily sorted out, though, as Beth's drugged compliance made it easy to convince her that everything was as it had always been. The television was the big problem: she wanted to know who had won the revived *Strictly Come Dancing* – Beth was a huge fan of Brucie 2 – and was desperately disappointed to miss Jeremy Clarkson 39 in *Top Gear Redux*. Privately, Nick was relieved that he would miss another three months of that; Clarkson had become positively reckless since his first replication, setting a bad example to youngsters both rich and poor, and single-handedly initiating a major surge in road traffic accidents.

Other than that it all seemed to be going smoothly. Beth's body operated as it was supposed to do, as far as Nick could tell. She could walk, talk and do all the things she used to do without additional or missing body parts causing problems. She ate, drank and carried out her toilet functions in the traditional manner. She liked all the entertainments she liked before her first death, and held the same opinions. The drugs helped enormously, of course;

but she seemed to be settling down nicely. She did seem to fart rather a lot, but Nick thought that was probably down to the exotic foods she was eating.

Beth's diet did worry Nick. She itched to go shopping, something Nick was hopeless at. Indeed, he *wanted* her to shop, because that would at least mean he would get some decent home cooking. Nick himself couldn't cook to save his life and whenever he went to Waitrose he invariably came home with all the wrong things in all the wrong quantities. He was just as bad when it came to online shopping. And with the internet out of bounds – he'd told her it was broken and being repaired – he relied on deliveries and carry-outs from the local restaurants. So they lived on curry and bento boxes, pizza and Chinese food. And although he yearned for a good roast, the story he'd spun Beth – that it was unsafe for her to go out because the streets were crowded with semi-feral homeless people since the Government had abolished all state benefits – kept her indoors until further notice. A few farts seemed a small price to pay for saving Beth from psychological trauma.

Nick never heard his wife fart, but the odour was unmistakeable. It seemed worse when she was doing the housework. Sometimes the smell was pretty foul but Nick had been brought up the old-fashioned way: ladies never farted and God help the man who told a woman that she did. So he put up with it.

The TPR manual that came with Beth 48 said that one should refrain from sex with the new model until the night before the counselling session – the idea being that the warm afterglow of love-making would put the replica in a more relaxed and pliable frame of mind, and thus make him or her more receptive to the news that they'd died. The three-month period of abstinence would, in theory, make the sex both very exciting and extra-satisfactory. Nick followed those instructions to the letter – he'd gone so long without it that going another three months without getting his leg over was a piece of cake. Consequently, when the time came, he was determined to make up for it.

At last, the big night came. Nick pulled out all the stops: candlelight and champagne, a top-notch gourmet meal ordered from Keith Floyd 2's takeaway franchise; romantic music – death had only temporarily interrupted Barry White's ability to rouse the ladies' passions, and his new album was said to be a sure-fire knicker-dropper – and several large bouquets of red roses. Beth was impressed. Nick was never quite sure if it was Barry White 2 or the oysters that tipped her over the edge, but they didn't even make it to the bedroom. And the sex was – unbelievable.

'I honestly couldn't believe it,' said Nick. 'I mean, it was bloody indescribable.'

The TPR company chief executive squirmed with embarrassment. 'Look, sir – you really don't need to go into detail.'

'Oh yes I bloody well do,' Nick retorted. 'She pushed me down onto the carpet and practically tore my clothes off. Then she did a striptease to Barry White 2's cover of "Sexual Healing" before slathering my private parts with the left-over chocolate-and-ginseng ice-cream. When she'd licked all that off, she mounted me like someone getting on a horse. And then – and then... Oh, God...'

'Sir, there's no need to tell me everything. I get the

picture, I really do.'

'She was insatiable,' Nick went on, ignoring the man. 'I mean, she was always a passionate woman. But she wouldn't let me get up. I was stuck there while she bucked away like a cowboy at a bloody rodeo. It went on and on and on. It felt like hours.'

The chief executive opened his mouth to speak again but Nick held up a hand in warning. 'Don't interrupt me. You have no idea what it's like to be in that position – helpless, unable to move, trapped while she wriggled and writhed on top of me. And what she did... I mean, I'm a broad-minded man, but I do have standards. It was disgusting.'

'I'm sorry, sir – I don't see what the problem is. Most men would be more than happy for their wives to be so – er – *enthusiastic* in their love-making. Between you and me, it sounds like you had a real result.'

'I had a result? Listen – up until that moment it had been going really well. I told you about the farting, didn't I? Well, that wouldn't have been a problem. I mean, we all fart, don't we? The trouble is, she hadn't been farting at all. That smell is what happens when Beth 48 *sweats*. My Beth has always sweated like a bloody pig during sex – frankly, until last night I'd always found that rather a turn-on – but now she smells like one too! Her bowels must be connected to her sweat glands or something. The stench was appalling and she wouldn't stop even when I threw up!'

'Sir, I can't apologise enough. The least we can do is fully reimburse you and throw in another try at TPR. Will that be satisfactory?'

Nick closed his eyes. If it had been anyone but Beth he

would have taken the money and resigned himself to yet another, longer period of mourning as he finally let her go for good. But it *was* Beth. He couldn't do it. He knew he would keep on trying until they got it right.

'OK,' he sighed. 'Let's give it another shot. To tell the truth, I'm getting pretty fed up with having to have her euthanised every couple of weeks, so I've decided to keep the next one come what may. After all, you're getting there, aren't you? As long as she works and there's no repeat of that last copy error it should be fine. I don't mind a few fingers too many – even the one with odd feet was alright, really. I mean, how bad could it be? I'm hardly likely to get one with tentacles and fangs, am I?' Nick forced a laugh.

Yes, how bad *could* it be? The chief executive thought of what had happened with H.P Lovecraft 2 and suppressed a shudder.

Et In Arcadia Ego

A couple of days ago I was in the big Our Price superstore in Manchester, checking to see what was new. Too much was, as usual, but that was brought into sharp focus by the conversation I overheard. Two boys in their late teens or early twenties – Londoners in Manchester for the university, going by their accents and mode of speech – were idly browsing the CDs and complaining about being bored. 'My life is just uninteresting,' one of the girls said to the other. 'I know exactly what you mean,' he replied. 'Every day is exactly the same as the one before. Nothing ever changes.' The young couple wandered off, holding hands. They didn't seem very enthusiastic about it, especially the girl.

Confused? You will be. I know I am, and it's been that way for quite a while.

One day in 1975 I unexpectedly found myself somewhere else. To be precise, I found myself in exactly the same place I had always been – but it was a different place.

I'd gone out for a walk, a spur of the moment decision. It was a nice, sunny Sunday morning in May and I felt like a spot of light exercise to set me up for the rest of the day. I was going to walk to the dual carriageway at the bottom of my street and cross to the fields and woodland on the other side. I like walking and I like nature. It seemed a lovely day to combine the two.

Halfway down the road I passed the opening to a cul-de-sac. I actually walked past it before turning back, puzzled. I didn't remember it at all, even though I'd lived in the same house for nearly twenty years and must have been up and down that road literally thousands of times. I knew the area like the back of my hand. As a kid I knew every short cut and hiding place in the area, every spot that might have been of interest to a bored, lonely kid who lived in fear of the local bullies. This place was wholly unfamiliar. Warminster Close, it was called. It had evidently been there for many years – the signpost needed a lick of paint, the trees were well-established, the houses clearly contemporary with the others in my neighbourhood.

I stood there and gazed vacantly at the houses. I had a good memory then as now and, as I say, an intimate knowledge of my environment. I didn't have the foggiest idea where Warminster Close had come from but I knew one thing with utter certainty. It hadn't been there the day before.

I walked slowly and apprehensively into the Close, half expecting to bang my nose against the wall of one of the houses that should have been there to block my way. That didn't happen, however. There were no unseen obstacles. When I trailed my hand along bushes and fences they felt solid and real. The cars parked there were warm with the sun when I touched them. The scent of roses and honeysuckle from the front gardens was sweet and powerful. I wasn't dreaming, I decided; and the sight was too consistent and natural to be a hallucination.

As I exited the close I experienced a sudden wave of vertiginous panic. What had become of Mr and Mrs Jenkins, my parents' friends, who lived in one of the houses that should have been there? Was I going mad? Had I somehow lost my memory and regained and regained only an incomplete version? I wanted to sit down on the pavement, shut my eyes and wish everything back the way I remembered it. I didn't sit down but actually did close my eyes. When I opened them the Close was still there.

Shocked into a state of numb disbelief, I returned home. My mother was sitting at the kitchen table with a cup of tea and the *Daily Mirror*. Had she been wearing that blue dress when I went out only ten minutes before? Yes, I was sure she had. I forced the words out.

'Mum, what happened to Mr and Mrs Jenkins down the road?'

She smiled distractedly, her attention fixed on the Old Codgers or Live Letters. 'Who did you say, dear?'

'Bill and Gladys Jenkins. What happened to them?'

Mum looked up at last, frowning slightly. 'I don't know them. Should I? Do they live round here?'

I didn't pursue it. I was too stunned. To my certain knowledge Bill Jenkins and my father had been going to the local pub together almost every Friday for years, and Gladys and my mother were thick as thieves. Now my mum was sitting there denying she even knew them. What on earth was happening?

Mum closed the newspaper, and as she did so I had

another shock. The front page news was about Manchester United's 3-2 victory over Bayern Munich in the European Cup final in Paris the night before. I knew for a fact that United had been relegated to the Second Division the previous summer and shouldn't even have been playing in the European Cup that season; and I'd actually watched the final live on television as Bayern beat Leeds United 2-0.

I retired to my room in a daze to collect my thoughts. Maybe some music would somehow put things back to rights? I was clutching at straws. But it got worse. Bowie's *Young Americans* LP had become a sprawling double album called *Shilling the Rubes*, crammed with tracks I'd never heard of. I played it anyway. The songs I knew sounded just the same. The others were wholly strange to me. Listening to this unheard material, I was so enthralled that for nearly an hour I forgot that it shouldn't exist. When I'd heard all the new songs I went through my records looking for further anomalies but finding none. I sprawled on my bed and lit a cigarette, trying desperately to get to grips with whatever was happening to me.

And that's when I had the really bad thought.

'What do you want?'

The voice was cool and neutral, not at all what I was expecting but pretty much what I'd been dreading. By that point my thoughts and feelings were all over the place. I'd learned that world had changed in all sorts of minor ways – minor to me, at any rate, though evidently other people's lives had diverged alarmingly from my memories of them. I would have to get used to it; they, on the other hand, already had. I was the one who had to adjust. But there was one thing I desperately needed to be the same as it had been.

'Are we still on for tonight?' I held my breath as I waited for the response. I'd been going out with Jean for just over six months and had recently realised that I was beginning to care about her quite a lot.

There was a short silence, followed by an exasperated clucking sound. 'I thought we'd finished with all this. It's over, Sam. It's been over for ages. Why can't you get it into your thick head that I don't want to see you again?'

'But Jean...'

'No, that's enough. If you phone me again I'm going to call the police. Do you understand? No more, Sam. I can't take any more.'

She hung up on me. I stared at the receiver, willing it to turn into a cucumber or something equally silly so I'd know it was all just a terrible, terrible dream. But no matter how hard I stared it continued to be a telephone.

The next day I went to my GP and told him what had been happening to me. He listened, with mounting concern, then gave me a physical examination. After that he told me that in general I seemed healthy enough, though he couldn't rule out brain damage or psychological illness. He was so matter-of-fact about it that I could have screamed at him. He noticed my growing agitation and referred me to the local hospital for an urgent assessment. For the NHS in those days 'urgent' meant at a snail's pace, but they seemed to take the doctor's referral seriously and I only had to wait six weeks before being seen. My head was hooked up to a machine that recorded my brainwaves, my blood and urine were sampled and tested, and my skull was X-rayed. I had to do a lot of seemingly pointless things like walking along a straight line and standing on one leg with my eyes shut. Lights were shone in my eyes, which were also tested and found to be as short-sighted as they had been at my last appointment with the optician a couple of months earlier. It was a few more weeks before I was called in to learn the results of this series of tests. Altogether it took them nearly four months to discover that there was nothing wrong with me. But of course, there was something not quite right; so I was referred to a psychiatrist.

The psychiatrist examined me again, asked me a lot of questions that I gamely tried to answer with a degree of honesty tempered with the knowledge that the truth might sound crazier than any fiction I could concoct. By this time *Young Americans* had returned to its old familiar self, though it was occasionally called *The Gouster* or *One Damn Song*. Warminster Close was still there. Manchester United appeared doomed to relegation to the Third Division, though. My occasionally ex-girlfriend phoned me every couple of days to ask why I'd dumped her, even though I never had. I did call her once, because I was lonely and missed her, and thought we might sort it out if she knew what I was going through. But she told me to piss off and stop pestering her. On a more mundane level, I sometimes still had a job when I went to work; at other times I didn't. My friends changed their drinking haunts and personal allegiances with bewildering speed, and pubs changed their names seemingly at random. Sometimes I was bafflingly broke; sometimes I was unexpectedly flush. Once I awoke with a dreadful hangover, though I was pretty certain that the previous evening I'd stayed in to watch *Tom and Barbara* – as *The Good Life* was called that night; somehow it wasn't as funny with Sid James as Tom – and had consumed nothing stronger than a cup of tea. According to my mother, however – she was now a red-head – I'd been to the cinema with my girlfriend and had come home wholly sober and waxing enthusiastic about Dennis Hopper's performance as Randle McMurphy in *One Flew Over The Cuckoo's Nest*. I'd seen that a week earlier with my mates and McMurphy had been played by Walter Matthau. Where I came from, all the advance publicity had been about Jack Nicholson but he wasn't even in it.

I really couldn't keep up.

One day I received a letter from the hospital, scolding me because I hadn't attended treatment for my brain tumour. When I meekly – and somewhat terrifiedly – kept the new appointment, the routine X-ray showed that the growth had miraculously disappeared. Of course, that was because it had never been there, as I knew full well. Or did I? I wasn't actually sure what I knew anymore.

Jean was having none of it. 'I don't care if you're not feeling well, Sam. We're going to Corfu next week no matter how bloody sick you are. I'm not losing the money I've paid out for this trip.'

Corfu? I didn't even know where that was. The furthest I'd ever been was a day trip to Calais when I was thirteen. Mind you, for all I knew Corfu could have been in Norfolk, perhaps even North London.

It was turning out to be a truly bizarre morning in what had become a very freaky life. Grandma Taylor was dead again; Manchester United had won the League Championship again, and Bowie had just announced a tour to promote his new album *The Visitor*, part of which was the soundtrack to Nicolas Roeg's new film *The Man Who Fell To Earth*, starring Mick Jagger. (Or Bowie himself, or Brad Dourif, or John Hurt, depending on what day it was. The next day the album was called *Station to Station* and half the tracks were missing.) Six Irish men charged with bombing a pub in Birmingham had been sensationally found not guilty when evidence of police corruption, brutality and falsification of evidence had come to light; or they had been given life sentences; or the pub had never been bombed at all – take your pick. To cap it all, Jean had turned up on the doorstep as if she was expected, sporting an engagement ring. For a minute I thought she'd come to vengefully taunt me with the evidence of new love, but it seemed I'd given her the ring a couple of weeks previously. This was news to me as only the night before I'd been on the receiving end of one of her increasingly-tearful telephone calls begging me to come to my senses and take her back. The day before that I'd taken receipt of an injunction that forbade me to phone her or go within a mile of her home. Whatever I did, I couldn't win.

Fortunately, my mother was there to calm things down. I left them chatting while I went upstairs to visit the toilet. When I got back, my mother was on her own, reading the *Daily Mail*.

'Where's Jean?' I asked.

'Jean? I don't know what you mean, dear. Isn't she going out with that Larry Turnbull now? She chucked you months ago, didn't she?'

My mother looked as puzzled as I felt. Normally the changes happened overnight, while I was asleep. This was the first time anything of the kind had occurred while I was up and about.

'It's OK, Mum,' I told her, smiling bravely. 'Just pulling your leg. I never want to see her again anyway.'

As I said that I realised it was true. I still cared about her but the constant switchback of our relationship was driving me crazy. I'd reached my limit. There was only one thing I could do.

I hate Manchester. I hate all the Manchesters, with their football teams that are never in the same division from one day to the next, their ever-changing punk bands and clubs and bars. I hate the job I sometimes have and sometimes don't; the flat that is sometimes nice and sometimes run-down and squalid; the women who like me one day and blank me the next; the semi-permanent friends I keep at arms length because I never know whether they'll buy me a drink or punch me in the mouth. I'll be moving on from here pretty soon – just as I moved on from Southampton, Leeds, Birmingham, Liverpool and everywhere else I've stayed in the decades that have passed since I left South London. I don't know where I'm going to go but I have an idea of what I'm going to do.

It was so long ago that I left home forever, so long that sometimes I forget how many years it's been. I call my mother occasionally, just to keep in touch with things that are pointless remembering. Sometimes she's dead and my father answers; sometimes it's the other way round; and quite often they're both still alive. Sometimes it changes in mid-sentence. Jean married Larry Turnbull, or Vinnie Dolan, or someone else, and has one, two, or three kids, and sometimes grandchildren. Jean has also died in a car crash, emigrated to Australia or become a local councillor. She's been and done other things, too.

I took a gamble and went to Corfu once, just to see what I'd missed. It was horrible, crammed with stupid, semi-naked youngsters out of their minds on ouzo and retsina, drunkenly trashing restaurants, stripping off in the streets and fornicating on the beaches, watched closely by vocally disapproving Greeks with one calculating eye on the profit margin. Corfu changed as frequently as anywhere else while I was there but it was always the bloody same. I never went back there, I can tell you.

There are so many places I can't go. I never know if I'd be going into a war zone or a haven of tranquillity. I'm skint sometimes, but just as often I'm moderately wealthy. I can't really plan ahead with any certainty. All I can do is throw some clothes and other possessions into a bag and hit the road, hoping they'll still more or less be the same when I arrive at my destination. That's been happening with increasing frequency. But I'm just over sixty now and I can't keep running. I'm feeling old, tired and worn down with anxiety and confusion.

I thought I might try to get to the United States again. The last time I tried was in September 2001, but my flight was cancelled when news came through about the nuclear attacks on Los Angeles, Washington DC, New York and Miami by Nicaraguan terrorists. When I woke up the next morning it had been a major nerve gas attack by a home-grown right-wing organisation based somewhere in

Montana. The following day it was claimed that some Muslims had been responsible for hijacking planes and flying them into the World Trade Centre and the Pentagon. Or it was the Japanese Aum cult, the Weathermen, Colombian drug cartels, Serb terrorists – I didn't bother trying to keep tabs on it after the first week, especially with President Bush/Gore/whoever making dire threats to nuke any nation not flying Old Glory from every rooftop, and Prime Minister Blair/Brown/Smith/Major/*et cetera* loudly standing shoulder to shoulder with whichever bug-eyed trauma victim was bunkered down in the White House at any given moment. There was one blissful morning when I awoke to find that 9/11 had been a normal, peaceful day when nothing much had happened but by then I'd lost interest in relocating to New York City.

I'm feeling increasingly afraid. Just lately I've been living in a permanent state of flux. One morning in the August of 2011 I went to work as usual, not knowing if they'd have even heard of me by the time I got there, and got off the bus to find the city in flames from a night of rioting that hadn't happened when I left home. When I entered the office ten minutes later the nation was in the grip of a full-scale civil war. I went out for a mid-morning cigarette and when I tried to get back inside the building had been occupied by colourfully-dressed students peacefully protesting against government cuts. It didn't really matter as my electronic building pass was no longer recognised. I decided to go home but the bus stop had become a monorail station and I couldn't read the timetable because it was in Cyrillic.

This morning I came to a final decision about my remaining years. I'm not safe anywhere I go, for the simple reason that I never know which where that would be. I still don't understand what has happened to me. My best guess is that I'm somehow slipping randomly from one parallel universe to another – unstuck in space, like Billy Christian/Pilgrim, the guy who was unstuck in time in that Kurt Vonnegut novel that is sometimes called *Slaughterhouse 5*. Or perhaps I'm suffering from some strange form of amnesia, in which I genuinely forget personal and global events and make it up as I go along, only to be shocked when I find my fantasy is nothing like the reality. All I do know is that I can't take any more of this bewildering cavalcade of uncertainties. I yearn for the days when I knew how much money I had and whose head was on it, whether or not I had a girlfriend, who the Prime Minister was, if I had a job, and if my parents were dead or alive. I long for the time when my record collection had albums with titles and songs I recognised, when I knew how my favourite football team was doing, and pubs had the same name for longer than ten minutes at a stretch. I crave those simple days. To me, that was a kind of paradise. For me nostalgia really is a pain because it hurts to have lost it all so completely.

I am going to the hospital, where I shall claim to be hearing insidious voices that are telling me to do terrible things. I shall even claim to have committed a few horrible crimes. There are always plenty of unsolved killings and the police are perpetually on the lookout for a suitable lunatic to collar for them. If I keep the details vague enough I should be in the frame for one or two. I'm going to dress the part – odd shoes and mismatched socks, suit trousers with a vest, an anorak – and have been practicing an array of tics, grimaces and other visual clues. I've done the research on the cloudweb or internet, e-space or whatever it might be called on the day, and I think I can be convincing. Besides, I know how eager the mental health professions are to label someone with this or that syndrome or personality disorder. You can't blame them for being a bit over-eager to lock someone up. It's their living, and you have to respect that.

By this time tomorrow I should be in a psychiatric unit, safely locked away from the ever-changing world, happy and warm in the arms of Largactil, Thorazine, Haloperidol or whatever else is the drug of choice in that particular establishment when I get there. I expect it'll be something different every day, but that doesn't worry me. All I want is to be someplace where I can dream that nothing ever changes, and be in a state where it doesn't matter a damn to me if it does. Sure, it'll be a kind of death – the death of a good deal of my personality, if what I've read about psychopharmaceuticals is any guide – but that'll be a sacrifice worth making. With any luck it'll also be the death of my fears and worries as I sink into the soothing haven of chemically-induced bliss. *Et in Arcadia ego*, and all that. At least I won't have to either inflict physical harm upon myself or return to bloody Corfu to escape my nightmare of inconstancy.

And who knows? I might end up in precisely the right place for me after all. Sometimes, as Siegfried Freud famously said, a banana is just a banana.

Pants

Timpson was pleased with his latest purchase. They were stylish. Available in a range of colours – from moody black to chaste white and encompassing passionate red, cool blue and sensible green – they looked just like boxer shorts. Yet they had the support and snugness traditionally associated with the discredited and derided Y-front. They were durable – each pair guaranteed to retain both colour and texture for at least five hundred washes – and, at thirty quid a pair, relatively inexpensive. And one size really did fit all.

Just to prove the point, Timpson took off his new Smartpants and put them on his head. The pants contracted to fit the new contours but – according to the selfie he took as evidence – they still looked exactly as a pair of boxers should. They were made of a new dual-layered 'smart' material that was self-adjusting for maximum comfort, eliminating those awkward and potentially painful moments when a change in posture or position might normally result in rucking or creases that chafed tender, intimate parts. Inbuilt thermostats controlled a system of irised pores and nano-cooling units that kept the internal heat constantly at a comfortable twenty degrees Celsius. The fly opened at the lightest touch of a finger. A firmer touch, at a particular location on the waistband, and they loosened and fell around the ankles. Obviously that didn't work when the Smartpants were worn on the head, so when he removed them Timpson was forced to hold them up to prevent them settling round his neck and throttling him.

The Smartpants didn't even cost anything to run. Power was provided by an innovative Freepower mesh battery woven into the fabric and recharged kinetically by the simple act of walking. The same mesh incorporated a Bluetooth connection that allowed for wireless firmware upgrades. They had originally been called iFronts but the threat of legal action involving the world's most expensive and lupine lawyers had scuppered that idea. Within six months of being launched, they had made their designer an eight-digit fortune, a good part of which was down to Timpson's acquisition of twenty pairs of the undergarments.

Yes, Gerald Timpson was very pleased with his Smartpants. But he didn't care what they were called. He had long suffered the torments of poorly-designed and ill-fitting mass-produced underwear – the embarrassing sweatiness, testicular claustrophobia and painful rubbing associated with Y-fronts, and the lack of support offered by boxer shorts. Worse still, he had a low sperm count, which according to his doctor was almost certainly down to years of overheating in the crotch region. The Y-fronts had to go, said his wife, whose body-clock was sounding the alarm increasingly loudly as the years passed – though to be strictly accurate it was the missus sounding the alarm as she fretfully ticked away the remaining seconds of her reproductive capability. Boxer shorts were no use – they didn't cook the gonads like Y-fronts or briefs but neither did they protect his private parts from either friction or Newton's Third Law of Motion.

The Smartpants were better than a blessing. Timpson wore them with pride and no small sense of relief. No more malodorous perspiration; goodbye to restriction and constriction; and farewell to those unpleasant red marks around the waist and at the junction of his thighs. Cool, unfettered yet in control, Timpson would be forever ready for action. Timpson had plans. And he'd chosen red ones.

Mrs Timpson was unaware of her husband's plans, which centred upon Muriel, his manager's swivel-hipped PA; or perhaps Linda, the voluptuous barmaid at the Wetherspoons he occasionally visited after a hard day at the office. It wasn't that Timpson had any burning desire for infidelity. Indeed, in twelve years of marriage he had never been unfaithful. It was merely that he yearned for a life of uncomplicated, carefree and joyful sex that wasn't dictated by the calendar, thermometers and optimum positions for conception. If he was brutally honest, he might confess to finding his wife's mechanistic approach to sex more than a bit off-putting. There wasn't much fun in it anymore. Georgina appeared to regard him as nothing more than a highly-ineffective sperm donor. It would probably be just as fulfilling for both of them with a copy of *Fiesta* and a turkey-baster. At the least the porn mag wouldn't drag him screaming from his slumbers for a shag when Georgina's latest get-pregnant scheme required his participation.

So Timpson enjoyed his new-found genital comfort and fantasised about happier times and just about every attractive woman he laid eyes on. For a couple of weeks his life was blissful. He chatted up Linda the barmaid, flirted with Muriel the PA and even Marjorie next door, whose husband was a long-distance lorry driver and who was rumoured to be free and easy with her favours after a couple of glasses of Chardonnay. Soon, he thought, he would make his move.

Then, sixteen days after the Smartpants had miraculously transformed his life, the balloon burst.

'How was the pub?'

'Pub?' How did she know he'd been to the pub? He'd only had an orange juice with soda, so there was no way she could smell booze on his breath. All he'd done was sit and ogle Linda the barmaid for fifteen minutes while pretending to do the *Times* crossword.

Georgina looked up from her Nexus 7. She didn't look at all happy. Nothing new there, but she wasn't usually quite *that* frosty. 'The pub,' she repeated. 'The Man in the Moon, or whatever it's called. The one we went to before the theatre a couple of months ago – the one with the barmaid.'

'Barmaid?'

'Is there an echo in here? We must get the acoustics sorted. Yes, *barmaid* – you know, the one with the tits and arse. I'm sure you remember. Your eyeballs were practically superglued to her buttocks.'

'Um – I don't know what you mean.'

She rolled her eyes. 'Do you know, you have a partial erection every two minutes on average, and a full erection every five minutes. The last full one was at fourteen minutes past five, ten minutes after you normally leave work. I will take it as read that you weren't walking around at the time, otherwise you'd probably still be explaining yourself at Charing Cross police station. Do you really think about sex *that* often?'

'Georgina, I don't know where you're getting these ideas, but...'

'Don't interrupt, Gerald. At three minutes past two this afternoon you were stroking yourself – you know where I mean – for precisely six minutes and twelve point seven seconds. I assume you were in the toilet while that was going on because I can't see them allowing you to do that at your desk in an open-plan office.'

Timpson did the only sane thing open to a man in his position. He lied. 'Er – I had an itch and I was scratching. You know me, I've always been a bit sensitive down there.'

'Really?' Georgina's eyebrows were raised but her expression was stony. 'I would have thought scratching would require a little more pressure than that but I shan't argue the point. I'm sure it was nothing to do with that Muriel with the short skirts.'

Timpson was relieved. He'd got away with it, though he was more than a bit rattled by mention of Muriel. But the respite was only temporary.

'Anyway, I thought your new Smartpants would have eliminated itching completely. No more sweating or chafing, remember? But even that doesn't explain what happened this morning at seventeen minutes to eight.'

'Seventeen minutes to eight?'

'That echo's back again. If I might be allowed to refresh your memory, at eighteen minutes to eight you left home for work. One minute later you had a partial erection.

Coincidentally, I happened to be looking out of the window to see if it was raining and I saw Marjorie next door bending over to pick up the milk. She was wearing that black negligee. Doesn't leave much to the imagination, does it? I also saw that you were standing on our doorstep checking that you'd remembered your wallet. That *was* what you were doing, wasn't it?'

Timpson nodded dumbly. How did she know about his erections, partial or otherwise? How did she know what he'd been up to in the office lavatory? How on earth did she *know*?

'Oh well, I suppose I'll just have to take your word for it. Still, at least you appear to have spent most of the day in a state of near-permanent sexual arousal. That's good, because I calculate that in about ten minutes I'll be at my most fertile for the month. So get your skinny arse up those stairs and get your kit off. I am *ready* to conceive and you'd better be up to scratch by the time I get up there. Oh, by the way, how are the new spectacles?'

'Spectacles? Um, they're fine, thanks.'

Georgina smiled, as dazzling and cold as an Antarctic ice shelf. 'Good. Go on, upstairs, now.'

Panic-stricken, Timpson took the stairs at a run.

Georgina returned her gaze to the tablet. Her smile did not diminish but it lost its chill. Technology was really amazing nowadays. She didn't understand how her thirteen year old nephew had managed to hack into Gerald's Smartpants, nor how he had programmed the tablet to create 3-D images of the Smartpants showing every move and twitch Gerald's parts made in the course of the day. Nor did she know how the boy had managed to insert a near-microscopic webcam into Gerald's spectacles so she could match what her husband saw with what was going on inside those Smartpants. Fortunately, the kid had an IQ that could have doubled as a telephone number, only left his bedroom to reluctantly go to school, and was easily bribed with a fifty-quid Amazon voucher, no questions asked.

She rewound the displays and once again watched Marjorie bending over the milk bottles, the corresponding bulge in the image of Gerald's pants. She didn't really blame Gerald. The woman really did have a nice bum. The sight of those succulent buttocks through the virtually transparent material was a definite turn-on. Not for the first time, Georgina wondered if she might be batting for the wrong team.

Now that was an idea. Perhaps if tonight's efforts came to nothing she could tempt Marjorie into a threesome? The excitement might fire poor old Gerald up a bit and put some much-needed lead in his pencil. Just as long as he fired his hopefully-live rounds into the right target, of course. She made a mental note to stock the fridge with a couple of bottles of Chardonnay. And just to be on the safe side, she would slip her nephew another fifty to figure out a way to send *commands* to Gerald's Smartpants – nothing too ambitious or destructive, just the ability to give his testicles a warning squeeze if he looked like getting a bit *too* frisky.

Carrot and stick, that was the way to do it.

The Tiger's Birthday

And so, as I sleep, some dream beguiles me, and suddenly I know I am dreaming. Then I think: this is a dream, a pure diversion of my will; and now that I have unlimited power, I am going to cause a tiger.
Jorge Luis Borges, *Dreamtigers*

Creatures like that did not belong in English woodland. She padded silently by the bushes where I was concealed, those black and gold stripes melting her into the sunlight lancing between trees, the burning eyes scouring away shade to find what was hidden within. I held my breath as she passed and my heart pounded when she stopped to sniff the air mere feet from where I stood. Then she seemed to shudder and her flanks rippled as she walked on and disappeared into the foliage.

It was ordinary English woodland – birch, holly and ash; bluebells and ferns; shrews, hedgehogs and mice, foxes and badgers; thrushes, blackbirds and wood pigeons. She did not belong there. There was no way she could have been there.

I followed anyway.

I'd been having versions of the same dream every night for nearly a year, a dream of a tigress stalking me through the deciduous woods near my home, a place I often visited. Once, when I was young, every now and then I walked there for pleasure; but lately I went there almost every day because losing myself among the labyrinth of mossy trunks and holly prickles was one of the few things that would ease my soul. I've never been particularly interested in nature, except as a consumer, one who experiences rather than knows it. All I've ever really known or cared about nature is that it makes me feel better when I'm out and about and surrounded by it. You don't think too much about the chemistry of aspirin when you take a couple of pills for a headache.

It's easy to get lost when you're already lost. My life had become an empty thing, a place of no directions or landmarks, a formless landscape where maps and destinations were meaningless. It didn't matter to me that I didn't know where I was or where I was going. Anywhere was the same as anywhere else. I'd come to a dead end that had no limits, a cul-de-sac that seemed to go on forever.

That's the way it was for me for quite a while – years of aimlessness and bone-deep sorrow that refused to go away, a life I no longer wanted but lacked the will to end. I just carried on from one day to the next, walking in my soothing woods in all weathers but going nowhere at all until the days became weeks and months and the sun returned again and again to the same place in the sky. It wasn't really a life at all, I suppose, more a kind of unsatisfying slumber. But I had nothing else.

Then the tiger came.

When I woke the morning after that first dream I felt different, somehow warmer, as if the sun had risen in my soul after a long, cold night. My heart was beating fast and my lips hinted at something like a smile for the first time in an age. I could see her in my mind's eye, every detail sharply defined and clear: the eyes like globes of amber fire, the moist velvet of her nose as it twitched at my scent, each black or gold hair in stark relief. I could almost feel the muscles moving beneath her coat and smell the sweet stink of her breath. She was power and beauty, fascination and terror, fused together and crystallised in that luminous frame. She was dangerously gorgeous.

That cool May morning I went out to the woods with a kind of joy I had never known before. Walking through the trees was strange. I couldn't work it out at first but eventually I realised that I felt like I used to on outings when I was a kid, as if I was having an adventure. Every shadow and every bush or stand of trees seemed to hold promise and dread in equal measure. What was that shape I thought I glimpsed from the corner of my eye? Was there something crouching just out of sight, perhaps something camouflaged and blending with the wood and leaves? When would it emerge from cover and show me what it was?

I stayed in the woods for hours, hardly daring to move in case it broke the mood of anticipation. Nothing happened, of course. Not that day, nor the next. But each night I dreamed of the tiger and every day I went out to the woods and returned home filled with apprehensive wonder.

Gradually, the dream changed. Whereas at first I was

merely an observer, a disembodied mind watching the tiger prowling purposefully through the trees, sometimes sunning herself in a clearing or drinking from a stream, little by little I became more of a participant, more corporeal. I knew the tiger sensed my presence, that she was aware of where and what I was. I was sure she knew me intimately, in that way animals learn so much about one another by scent alone. She showed no outward sign that she was interested in me, though she must have been curious. She merely went about her business, whatever that was.

One night I was, as usual, following the tiger's trail in my dream. I pushed cautiously through some bushes and suddenly found myself face to face with her. I froze, terrified by that majestic, feral countenance, mesmerised by those fiery eyes that gazed calmly into mine. For the first time I felt that she was interested in me after all. But she turned and glided away through the trees and left me alone and shaking.

After that we met often, though for a long time she never acknowledged my presence. Sometimes the tiger and I would walk together, side by side, through the woods. It felt almost companionable but she paid me no attention. More often we would continue our strange game, her travelling on those unfathomable errands while I tracked her.

As the dreams evolved, so did my woodland walks. I began to feel that unseen presence more strongly. I began to imagine that the tiger was real. Was that a tuft of golden felid hair caught on a twig? What was that moving on the edge of my vision? Random marks on the ground were transformed into fragmented paw-prints. I felt uneasy yet enthralled by those ghostly traces.

One hot summer day, I wandered further than usual, into unfamiliar territory. I came upon a derelict house, all warped wood and sagging tiles, flaking paint and broken glass. I found a faded memory of it from my childhood – then it had been already old but well-maintained, curtains at the windows and flowers in pots on the sills, a home. Now the door was hanging half off its hinges, the floorboards visible within covered in leaves and wind-blown rubbish. It was a sad thing, a shell without the snail.

At the foot of the overgrown garden there was a small river, really a stream that hadn't quite grown up. On the far bank the trees thinned as the land rose. There were houses at the top of the rise, inhabited dwellings. I could hear distant music and children's voices as they called to one another. Then the noises abruptly stopped and the world was still and quiet. Above the houses the empty blue sky seemed to twist and ripple – it was surely an optical distortion caused by thermal currents but to me it seemed as if some vast, invisible being was moving there, something with gigantic wings beating and forcing at the atmosphere, an angel or perhaps a dragon. It was certainly dragon weather.

Laughing quietly at my own fancy I turned back to look at the old house, which now looked vaguely like an old, ruined face. On impulse, I followed the path to the front door. This place should have at least one ghost, I told myself as I entered.

As I roamed those empty rooms I realised that I was now one of those ghosts, a man who had given up on life because living had become too painful to bear. That ghost was haunted by another. I sat on the floor of what had once been a bedroom and listened to the house's noises. A muffled rattle above my head suggested starlings or a squirrel on the roof. Quiet scratching indicated mice. The tired wooden frame creaked irregularly as the building warmed up in the afternoon sun. I rested my head against the peeling wallpaper and drifted away, remembering things that I was surprised to find weren't as bad as they had once seemed. I think I was even smiling at some of them. Then the low growl I hadn't even noticed mutated seamlessly into a throaty purr.

No longer drowsy, I sat perfectly still, my eyes wide and ears straining to hear what the owner of that purr might be doing. Soft footsteps came from downstairs, a loud exhalation, then silence. I was afraid but I wasn't scared.

Minutes passed. They seemed like hours. I stood as quietly as possible and, holding my breath, crept down the decaying staircase. At the foot of the stairs I stopped. I could hear and see nothing out of the ordinary but I could smell her. Her scent, musky and sweet with pheromones, overpowered the house's stench of mildew and rot. I shook my head and smiled again. My imagination was getting out of control.

Early in the spring the game changed again. Perhaps my presence in the dreams had become more substantial, to the point where the tiger could no longer pretend I wasn't there. Or maybe she was simply bored with the docile English woodland in my head and needed to sharpen her hunting skills on something more interesting, more challenging than rabbits and pigeons. Perhaps she was simply getting hungry. She began to follow me, tracing my scent and padding along silently in my footsteps, seeking me in the shadows and shrubs. It was subtly done. One moment I was watching and following her; the next she was doing the same to me. I didn't even notice when it happened. Oddly, I didn't think I was in any danger. We were playing a complicated game, moving in a circle that expanded and contracted but never quite closed. The rules were hers and I didn't really know what they were or understand the object of the game, but I played along. On reflection, perhaps it wasn't really a game at all but was a kind of dance. I wondered if it was a courtship ritual. It was not, I admit, wholly without eroticism; but more importantly my attachment to the tiger was becoming intensely emotional.

The tiger dreams were echoed in the real world – though perhaps that had never been quite as real as I'd assumed it was, not as far removed from the realms of dream as I'd always believed. In my local charity shop, usually a cheap source of the dog-eared thrillers and crime novels that whiled away my time, I found a near-pristine copy of Borges' *Dreamtigers*. A few weeks later, the same shop provided matching framed prints of Henri Rousseau's *Tiger in a Tropical Storm* and *Jungle with Tiger and Hunters*. I returned to the derelict house by the river and just inside the front door was a creased page ripped from a book of poems – *The Tyger* by William Blake. Every television documentary seemed to be about tigers; every shop I visited seemed to have Foreigner's *Eye of the Tiger* blaring out. Tigers stared at me every time I opened a magazine or newspaper. An old friend interested in the healing properties of crystals sent me a present of a golden-brown striated gemstone he said would help give me a more positive attitude – the stone was, of course, a Tiger's Eye. On my walks and everyday errands – now conducted with a spring in my step, a far cry from the stooped, defeated shuffle I had grown into – I would find small tins of Tiger Balm, scraps of tiger-striped wrapping paper, plastic toys and children's lost stuffed Tiggers. I began to collect them, hoarding my trophies in biscuit tins and cardboard boxes, on shelves and in drawers.

There were many such coincidences and chance finds. I was plagued by tigers. The more obsessed I became with the tiger, the more enamoured of her, so the coincidences increased. The plague became an epidemic that swelled as she seared herself into my soul. Unlike the tigers of Borges' dreams, mine was no parody or tawdry imitation. My tiger was a wild, black and golden flame: burning bright.

I rose shortly before dawn. It was one year exactly since my first dream of the tiger – and it had been the first night since then that I hadn't dreamed of her. I had eagerly anticipated it as a day of celebration, the birthday of renewed purpose and interest in life, but instead I felt bereaved, as lonely and aimless as I had been before she came. That refreshed emptiness was intolerable and I had to do something about it. I quickly washed and dressed and made my way to the woods, the only solace I could call upon.

Even that early in the morning the place was alive with insects and small mammals rustling and scurrying in the undergrowth and branches, birds feeding and calling to one another. Nature is rarely peaceful, and that tiny cacophony told me that for nature it was business as usual. On the surface it was as it had always been. Yet something was different – the woods were occupied by something terrible and alien but which I knew intimately. I knew that as soon as I passed between the first trees and primal fear thrilled along my spine. Nothing was obvious to my eyes and ears but my blood and marrow whispered a warning that was also a promise. I could smell her.

The lesser carnivores and small mammals weren't alarmed. Why should they be when they were not big enough to attract the interest of a large predator? The birds likewise carried on as they always did, focused solely on seeds, insects and grubs, with only a fraction of their attention on danger. This was English woodland, and for native birds danger usually came from the air, not the ground.

But there was danger for me. I could feel her as surely as I could feel a flame about to burn me. How she had got there, transported from my dreams to the world of flesh and bone, tree and stone, I don't know. Yet it was so. The tiger awaited me. It was impossible but true.

By then it was too late. I was in territory she had come to know well from her nightly sojourns in the scenery conjured by my sleeping mind. This had become her familiar hunting ground, her territory as much as it was mine. And now she was real, she would be different. This time she would not be an aloof companion or enigmatic playmate; she would not be a thing of wonder and beauty for me to observe. This time she would be a huntress.

Instinct kicked in and terror flooded my body with adrenaline as I turned and began to run. I couldn't help myself – it was an ancient reaction that was deeply imprinted in my DNA and could not be overridden. And it was a mistake. Tigers, I had learned from the endless stream of television documentaries, preferred to stalk and take their prey from the rear. Even as I recalled that and tried to halt my headlong flight, I heard the heavy thud of paws running up behind me and something struck my back, forcing me down hard.

I was on my hands and knees, my head bowed. I could feel her weight on me as those lethal jaws clamped around my neck, warm saliva flowing from her mouth to the nape and running onto my downturned face. Her teeth gently pricked my skin, drawing tiny droplets of blood I could sense but not see. She was purring loudly as she inhaled my scent and exhaled gusts of sweet, intoxicating breath around my trapped head. Her heartbeat was an echo of the wild drumming in my chest.

In that moment I felt wholly alive again. I thought perhaps she wouldn't hurt me, though it didn't matter if she did. I would be alive as never before, even if she tore me apart and feasted on my innards. My heart was hers anyway, and now she had come to take it, her birthday gift. We had come together at last, and there was nowhere I would rather have been. I belonged to the tiger as surely as the tiger belonged to me. The hunted and the huntress were one.

I closed my eyes and prayed she would never let me go.

Walkin' Back to Happiness

He was too old for this, much too old. Knees creaking and aching, muscles weak and weary from standing and walking, pavement-abused feet that felt like two slabs of sweaty corned beef – he was wearing sturdy walking boots that had been comfortable an hour ago but were now blistering his toes and baking his poor old plates alive – all the symptoms of being much too bloody old for this lark. And the bloke droned on and on, getting it all wrong. Like all modern 'experts' the man had discounted Martha Tabram. Historians weren't what they used to be, and that was a fact.

He could say the same about himself. The clock and calendar had been kind and he'd kept on working into his late seventies but now he was too old for all this walking. It was all down to wear and tear. People simply weren't designed to live far beyond their three-score and ten, not with any degree of comfort at any rate. He was an old man and suffering the pains of age, even though he liked to keep himself fit with gentle exercise and took pride in his appearance, spry for his years, a twinkle still in his eye when he spied a pretty girl – and by God, the girls nowadays were not only pretty but many wore those newly fashionable garments that left very little to the imagination, miniskirts they were called.

He still wasn't sure what he thought about that. Like any other red-blooded male he enjoyed the sight of a shapely female leg, the soft curve of a thigh. But those sights had their time and place; they should be things women shared with men in private, behind drawn curtains and closed doors. He disapproved of women publicly showing themselves off like that, flashing their drawers for anyone to see whenever they bent over. He remembered the sensation 'topless dresses' had caused a couple of years earlier. That had revolted him. How could any self-respecting woman parade around with her breasts on display? There were words for women like that.

They were on the fourth site now, location of the second part of the famous 'double event', the place where Catherine Eddowes had inhaled her last breath of air and expended the last of her blood. The bloke had introduced himself as a historian. Some bloody historian. He was making so many mistakes it was difficult to believe he'd ever read a book in his life. He'd named the first victim Mary Jane Nicholls, the second had been Alice Chapman and the third was supposedly Elizabeth Pride. The fool had got every date wrong. Not one killing had been described accurately. The old man wanted to correct him but held his peace. He was anonymous, only a face in a crowd, and that was just the way he liked to be – unnoticed and therefore unseen.

This was the fifth time he'd returned to London since he left for South Africa all those years ago, Durban by way of New York City, Mexico and Spain, France and Italy, a few other countries. The first time had been for the FA Cup final in 1923 – that had been a cracking occasion, all the supporters spilling onto the pitch and that copper on the grey horse trying to keep order. His team had lost two-nil to Bolton Wanderers but he'd had a splendid time. This was his third visit in consecutive years – he'd been to the Cup Final again in '64, this time seeing his beloved Hammers victorious against Preston North End – three-two, with goals from John Sissons, Geoff Hurst and Ron Boyce. Last year he was back at Wembley for the European Cup-Winners' Cup final against TSV 1860 München, sealed by a brace from Alan Sealey. Glory days! And just a few days ago he had been at Wembley for the fourth time to see England beat West Germany. Really, it had been another Hammers victory – Moore, Peters and Hurst had been the heart, brain and muscle of the team, and Hurst's hat-trick would live forever in the nation's memory. Fair enough, the other players had been more than adequate – Bobby Charlton and Roger Hunt had both flair and work-rate, and would look the part in the famous claret and blue – but it was the Irons' day. His team had won the World Cup for England. He swelled with pride at the thought.

His team? Well, only in a manner of speaking, if he was honest. West ham United hadn't existed when he left London. He'd adopted them as his team because they were the only decent team near to his birthplace. Supporting the Orient had never been an option. A posh boys' club, formed by students from Cambridge – how could he ever think of Orient as his local side? Anyway, they hadn't adopted the name until the year he left London and he hadn't even heard of them until long after he'd become a West Ham supporter. Football might be a global game but in those days news travelled slowly. He followed West Ham in the newspapers and on the wireless but the only times he'd ever seen their players in action were those special occasions. Back in South Africa he'd been starved of football until 1959, when the Durban City club was formed as part of the new National Football League. He enjoyed going to their games – as well as the football it was an opportunity to be a face in a crowd again, with the bonus of not seeing a single black face. Like rugby and cricket, South African football was blessedly *kaffir*-free. It was a far cry from London, where blacks seemed able to come and go as they pleased, wherever and whenever they wished. Like many other British emigrés, he had no great love of the Boer but he had to admit that apartheid was one of their better ideas.

Politicians and do-gooders might think London had improved in the twentieth century but he knew better. There were still slums and red-light districts, gangsters and poverty, low-life criminals preying on those who already had next to nothing. White women were sleeping with black men – he'd seen the evidence in prams and push-chairs. There were still bombsites left over from the Luftwaffe raids, ruins that hadn't been touched in the twenty-odd years since they'd been created, for God's sake. Swinging London? The place was nothing more than a gift-wrapped turd and he hated it more with every visit. And now the city was crawling with blacks and Asians, young men strutting like peacocks with long hair and effeminate clothing, and young women dressed like the denizens of a whore-house.

At least they were relatively well-behaved. The night-time streets were no longer infested with women so drunk they could hardly stand, shouting obscenities, spewing their guts up and hoisting their skirts to urinate in the gutter, not caring who saw what. That was something he was glad had gone forever.

Apart from those football-related visits he'd only come back on one other occasion, to join up in 1915. He had been ready and willing to kill Germans for King and country. It was men's work and by then he'd been a man for a very long time. When he was thirteen years of age he'd decided for himself that he was a man, an adult. It was good enough for the Jewish boys in the surrounding streets, so why not him? He was big for his age, tall and strong, a man in all but the legal sense. A man does a man's work, and he'd begun the day after his thirteenth birthday. He'd been happy in his work and continued to ply his trade in New York, Mexico City, Paris, Rome and Madrid. In South Africa he'd worked among the poor blacks – yes, he was what they nowadays called a racialist, but his work was colour-blind, transcending international boundaries. In Belgium and France he plied his trade with enthusiasm, as the Hun could testify. It wasn't quite the same but it kept him happy, especially when he gave the locals the benefit of his expertise. Until his retirement he'd been happiest when he was working, and never happier than when he worked among his own people, which was only natural.

He found himself humming that song that had come out a few years ago, by that strangely pretty Jewish girl, Helen Shapiro. It had been the top-selling record in South Africa for a while, always on the wireless, a real foot-tapper.

And what a voice! He'd read that the singer had only been fourteen when she recorded it. He didn't care for her hairstyle but the girl could certainly belt out a tune. She was an East Ender, like himself. Born in Bethnal Green, he'd heard. He hoped success hadn't spoiled her, that the strong Jewish morality he remembered from the East End of his youth still held sway and the temptations of stardom would not lead her astray and into the sordid world of miniskirts and drugs, drink and promiscuity. He'd seen more than enough of that in his day.

Well, not the miniskirts.

He leaned on his stick, needing to take the weight off and flex his knees before they set like cement and made the resumption of walking an agony. The historian was winding up his mistreatment of Catherine Eddowes' demise and they were about to move on to whatever was left of Miller's Court and the dissection of Mary Jane Kelly, which he hoped would be treated more carefully and respectfully by the so-called expert. Sixpence, this guided walk had cost – money for old rope, practically a give-away to that buffoon who clearly hadn't done his homework. He wished he'd spent the money on a cup of tea and a ham roll instead. Still, it was nice to be out and about in his old haunts, even if they were now barely recognisable. Like little Mary Kelly after Jack had finished with her. But he couldn't see himself coming here again. This would be his last stroll down Memory Lane, so he was making the most of it.

Knuckles cracked and popped as he grasped the stick tightly to make sure he didn't lose his balance and fall onto the paving slabs. At his age a broken hip could put him out of action for months. That wouldn't do at all. Today was the sixth of August, his ninety-first birthday. Happiness was long gone but he had a bit more walking still to do.

Ringbanen

The beer is cold and golden and frothy, and exactly what I need tonight. This is my first, the one to drink slowly and savour. I'm sitting alone at a table in a nice little bar in a city I am beginning to know and understand. As cities go, this one is better than most I've been to. I wouldn't exactly say I feel at home here – that was something for another man in a life long ago – but it's welcoming in its way. Here I don't have that sense of being a germ, mobbed by antibodies, rejected and readied for expulsion. Here I can rest, think and get things into perspective. I can regroup. I can –

Well, maybe I can't do that. Not even here. God knows I've tried.

Sometimes I wander through the Nationalmuseet. The combination of eighteenth-century architecture, twentieth century refurbishment and twenty-first century technology was unsettling at first but after the first couple of visits it seemed a natural environment for artefacts from all periods of the country's history. I'm not especially interested in the exhibits. I'm attracted by that juxtaposition of past times, the way the illusion of temporal flow is simultaneously suspended and maintained. I have no real interest in how people lived in ancient times, no sense of what they thought, felt or believed. What they did is irrelevant except insofar as it got us to here and now, whatever that means. Great historical treasures such as the Gundestrup cauldron or the Trundholm Sun Chariot, the rune stone in the museum courtyard, are merely objects. Whatever significance they may once have had eludes me.

The one thing that does draw me every time is the woman. That tanned-leather skin that was once soft and warm, that perhaps shivered to a lover's touch, the empty sockets that once held eyes blue and shining happily or moist with tears, the mouth now forever open in what might be a scream of agony, a shout of defiance or even a gasp of passion.

The Huldremose woman was found in Jutland in 1879. She died more than two thousand years ago, laid to rest in a peat bog, placed there with respect and love, dressed in a long, colourful woollen plaid skirt, a nettle-fibre petticoat, a scarf and two sheepskin capes, a comb and a headband. A woollen dress, presumed to be her property, was later found nearby. A length of rope was tied around her neck. Was she a criminal, hanged and disposed of still wearing the rope that took her life? Was she ritually strangled, a sacrifice to the gods thought to dwell in the otherworld beneath the water's surface? Was the rope merely an ornament, a kind of necklace, and not the instrument of her demise?

Even though I can't help wondering, the reasons for and mode of her departure from this life are irrelevant to me. After two millennia I doubt they mean much to her either. She is dead and that's all there is to it. Looking at that distorted, discoloured corpse – the bones softened, dissolved and vanished long before she was returned to this surface world – it would be easy to forget she was once alive. Yet I cannot forget it. The fact that her body was treated with dignity is what matters to me. I know someone cared about her. She was loved. Does anything matter more?

I wonder what her name was.

I live by writing – freelance journalism, travel and culture for magazines, newspapers and websites, with the odd short story under a name that isn't mine. It's not a bad living. I'm not fabulously wealthy but I'm not poor. I came here after Amsterdam, to write that novel I'd always known I had in me and by doing so purge my system. So far I haven't written a single damned word. I fritter my time away drinking and walking, thinking but rarely talking.

On sunny days I go down to the harbour, drink Carlsberg in the bars there, listen to the Swedes over for the day for a cheap piss-up. I don't speak much Swedish but I can understand some of what they say. I can't figure Danish out at all, though. The Swedes say the Danes speak as if they have their mouths full of pickled herring. I won't argue with that. The written language is fine but I find the spoken variety incomprehensible and unpronounceable, the vowels and consonants merging and twisting into a kind of prolonged, rhythmic groan. But it isn't disagreeable and I like the Danes. They're polite, kind and sometimes joyously loud, especially when they've had a few beers. Most of them speak excellent English, thankfully. It makes getting drunk here much easier than it might otherwise be. And they're good people to get drunk with, usually.

I get drunk a lot. It doesn't stop me thinking about that woman in the glass case, or why I think of her so often, but it makes the thinking more tolerable. Carlsberg here isn't like it is at home. There are more varieties on offer and even the familiar brew is a bit stronger and definitely more palatable. I took a tour of the brewery once, got my free drink and had a couple more, which set me up nicely for a desperate, amnesiac night in the little bar next to my apartment. I live just south of Grøndal station, on the S-tog's yellow-coded line, the Ringbanen. Technically I don't live in Copenhagen at all but in the autonomous municipality of Fredriksberg, which was never incorporated into the Danish capital, though it is entirely surrounded by it. It's a good residential neighbourhood, a mixture of old and modern buildings, just far enough from and close to any place of interest. The rent is lower than I would be paying in London for a fully-furnished flat and it's all-inclusive. There's the bar and a couple of others close by, the bakery, a Netto, a bank with an ATM, and the station. It's pretty much all I need.

I never did find out why the Carlsberg brewery has those four elephants at the gate. Maybe the designer was inspired by ancient Oriental cosmology. Or perhaps it's to symbolise the memories that beer helps you forget. I don't know.

She was at least forty years old when she died. Her last meal had been rye bread. In life she'd broken a leg, but it had healed. She was looked after, cared for. The body had been cut so deeply that one of her arms was almost severed – there is some argument as to whether it happened shortly before she died or was done when her body was excavated from the peat. I'd go with the latter. It makes more sense. Her hair had been closely cropped, leaving only stubble to cover with that plaid scarf. Another sacrifice, to a deity pleased by the gift of hair? She had been blonde, her hair the colour of ripe corn. Perhaps the haircut had been an offering to ensure a good harvest, her head shorn to symbolise reaping. Who knows?

I wonder what her name was.

It's funny how so many good, pleasurable things are yellow. There's gold, of course, and sunshine, daffodils and crocuses and sunflowers, bananas, butter, cheese and mustard, lemon curd and custard, and the ripe grain that makes our bread and beer. And there's honey. We use that word as an endearment. Once upon a time beer was sometimes sweetened with honey. It can be fermented into mead, the drink offered to honoured guests in time long past. Like corn, honey is harvested – bees gather nectar from flowers and in turn people reap the insects' produce. Like corn it keeps us alive and can help us forget.

The beer helps me forget, for a while. But it also makes me remember.

The Copenhagen Interpretation of quantum mechanics was formulated by Niels Bohr and Werner Heisenberg in the late 1920s, at Bohr's Institute of Theoretical Physics. The interpretation holds that quantum mechanics does not describe objective reality but only subjective observations or measurement of energy quanta. As soon as you start observing light (for instance) it behaves as either a wave or a particle, depending on how you're looking at it. The act of observing causes it to assume only one of its possible forms or values. That assumption of one form to the exclusion of all others is known as the waveform collapse.

Memories are like that. You look at a certain memory and it seems to be one thing and that thing only. Look at it again on another day, in a different frame of mind, and it appears to be something very different. Take that memory you have, the one you treasure – the look in that woman's eye on that particular evening, that moment everything changed. What you see there is the light of love. A few days later you think of it again and it is only the sparkle of amusement at something you said. The next time it is a glint of amusement of a different kind – she is laughing at you. What were you that night – the loved one, the comedian or the dupe? Which do you believe? Which was true? Maybe they were all true. Or was the truth something else entirely?

Is there any such thing as truth, in anything at all?

The Institute of Theoretical Physics was partly funded by the Carlsberg Foundation. That didn't surprise me when I found out.

Each time you see it, the past is different – it depends on intention and state of mind. I'm doing it now, in this tacky bar filled with drunken Swedes, their faces painted blue and yellow, their national colours. Football supporters on their way home from a match somewhere, fortifying themselves for the trip across the Øresund bridge, to Malmö and beyond. They shout and sing, some good-naturedly, others mournfully. They are not obviously aggressive, though I sense that hostility is only an unintended insult or a sour thought away. A few beers from now, I shall be just like them. The only difference will be that the blue and yellow I wear internally will be, I hope, banished for a little while.

The music in this place is the usual meaningless pop drivel you hear in cheesy bars the world over. It is so loud it almost drowns out the noisy Swedes. I shall move on to another bar, a quieter bar, and have more beer. I will bleed myself dry of these memories that never stay the same.

Yesterday I pretended to be a tourist. I suppose that is indeed what I am, though I'm loath to admit it even to myself. My residence here is only temporary, after all, and I often roam the city sightseeing like any other visitor. Usually my journeys trace tantalising patterns in lines between one bar and the next – though to be honest, my drunken wanderings are as aimless as those of any drunk and if there is a pattern it is well hidden and I can't see it. On occasion, as yesterday, I stay sober and plan my itinerary, carefully choosing my destinations so I can get to know the city more intimately. On warm, sunny days when I am sober and people are happy Copenhagen feels like a fairytale land and I half-expect to see Danny Kaye singing 'Thumbelina' and dancing around the Dragon Fountain and the Hans Christian Andersen statue in Rådhuspladsen, or the inchworm measuring the marigolds in the flower beds of Kongens Nytorv. On days like that, like Hans, I let my heart speak. It tells me a different truth each time. Like the golden Weather Girl on the Richs building on the corner of Rådhuspladsen and Vesterbrogade, what it says depends on the prevailing mood. How will she appear today – on the bicycle or walking the dog and holding her umbrella? Sun or rain? Gloomy or bright?

Yesterday my heart said me and my arithmetic will probably go far. I won't count on it.

Armed with equations that gave a different result every time I made the calculations, I walked around the big square and by the fountain made a silent wager that the bull would one day beat the dragon. Rådhuspladsen is a favourite place for the locals to parade their children – men with facial hair proudly pushing baby-laden buggies, their indulgent women smiling at everyone. The men may have the beards but Danish women know who wears the trousers. I always smile back, though their happiness makes me ache.

Late in the afternoon I went to the Nationalmuseet again, to see that long-dead woman whose smiles are now not even a memory.

I have been travelling through time all my life, going from then to now and perhaps beyond. For the most part I move in the standard direction at the accepted speed – forward at the rate of sixty seconds per minute, sixty minutes per hour. What's ahead is largely unknown, though experience, expectation and the balance of probability allows me to make educated guesses that are sometimes more or less accurate. Now and again I travel backwards, from now to then, fixing on a particular moment and zeroing in, freezing and examining it from a variety of angles and viewpoints. As Heisenberg and Bohr would have predicted, and as I have already described, what I see is rarely as I remember it and every time I revisit one of those moments it is different to how I thought it was before and how it seemed after. The past is as uncertain as the future.

The Huldremose woman is similarly inconstant. Although I visit her often, at least three times a week, even if I had artistic talent I could never draw her from memory

– that distorted mannequin, a sculpture by Hans Bellmer re-imagined by Francis Bacon in the throes of *delirium tremens*, shifts in my mind like those other memories. The only thing that never changes is my instinctive recognition that she was loved.

I must leave this bar right now. The music has been turned up and the Swedes are singing along to that song I loathe. That colour fills my mind, blinding me with its glare. It's why I left Amsterdam so soon after visiting that museum on Paulus Potterstraat. Vincent's sulphurous chair, his sunflowers, the cornfield – the colours of diseased sunlight. Nothing made any sense there after that. The canals burned through my heart like rivulets of acid and those anorexic waterfront buildings made me nauseous. Within days I developed a constant migraine, my hands shaking and vision streaked with blinding flashes like darting canaries. The shadows and light of the Rembrandts and Vermeers in the Rijksmuseum were an inadequate analgesia. Amsterdam spewed me out like bile from a diseased gut. I landed here.

I don't think it would it make any difference if I knew where I was going. After all, I'm not quite sure where I've just been. All I know is that it was a small bar in a backstreet off Strøget – there was a tattoo parlour just around the corner, a sunken place with a life-sized skeleton sitting in a chair in the doorway. Some bearded bikers were hanging round outside, exchanging jeers and obscenities with a couple of goth girls, all black and purple clothing and hair framing white faces. It was a rough flirtation with a dangerous edge. I didn't stop to take in further details.

I need to relieve myself urgently. To my relief the next bar isn't too far and I make it to the lavatory without pissing in my jeans. I'm getting too old for this. The urine erupts from me in a jet of yellow, making the water in the bowl seethe and foam. It looks not unlike what I've been drinking all evening, as if the beer has passed through my body without being processed. I laugh at the thought and lose my balance as I zip up, banging my elbow hard and painfully against the cubicle door. I laugh at that too. I'm much drunker than I thought.

That's good.

There's a vacant stool at the bar. I cautiously shuffle my backside onto it, drunk enough to fall off it but not yet drunk enough not to care about falling on my arse in public, smiling politely at the woman next to me. She smiles back, as pissed as I am. I try but fail to order a beer in Danish. Not that it makes any difference – the barman knows my look and what I need. He's seen it a thousand times before in so many different faces. I gesture toward the woman and he nods then pours us a beer apiece. The woman raises her glass to me and I mirror the action. She is blonde, blue eyed. Of course she is. Good cheekbones and an inner sweetness I can almost taste. It's like travelling back in time.

Her English is excellent. When I remark on that she tells me she studied English at university and has travelled to New York and London many times. I make a few jokes and she laughs, genuinely – not the fake laugh of someone who wants to curry favour or set someone at ease. She does those little things that women do when they're interested in men, plucking a speck of lint from my jacket, lightly touching my hand when she wants to emphasise what she is saying, leaning close when I speak, so close that our faces almost touch. I tell her I'm a writer. She's interested, asks me a few questions – not the usual enquiries as to how much money I make or if I'm famous or where my stories have been published, but about how I establish character and motivation, how I dream up plots, how I think the imagination actually works. I'm impressed that she can think that way when she's so obviously several sheets to the wind, and I find myself hoping that my fractured replies aren't too much of a let-down. I ask her why an attractive, likeable woman like her is out drinking on her own. Not in so many words, of course.

She's quite open about it. She tells me she has come out to get drunk and, if she meets the right man, to get laid. Her boyfriend has cheated on her one time too many and she has told him to get the fuck out of her life. But now she's feeling sad and lonely. And drunk and horny, she adds with a brief, self-mocking grin. I start to laugh but stop when I see the way she is looking at me. No, I tell myself, I don't want this. I don't want to be a stunt man in a stranger's revenge fantasy. And I don't want her.

I finish my drink and she buys me another.

I wonder what her name is. But I don't ask.

It is late morning in an unfamiliar street in a part of the city I've never been to before. I'm making my way to where I think is a rail station. Last night I paid for a taxi after staggering with her from the bar toward København Hovedbanegård and realising halfway that we were both too smashed to walk the whole distance without falling on our arses, and it dropped us off near a rail station. It's Hellerup,

I discover – I have been here once before but on the other side of the railway line. Divisions are so easy to make.

It hadn't been so bad, all told. It had been so long I was almost surprised to learn that I still remembered what to do, especially considering how drunk I was. I don't know if she enjoyed it. When we'd finished she cried herself to sleep in my arms. Just as dawn was breaking she woke me with a glass of pineapple juice and apologised for having been upset. We talked for a while. I told her a little more about myself, carefully skirting the important things. She was a secretary in a government office, in her late thirties and afraid of growing old alone. The last boyfriend was only the latest in a string of bad choices. She was, she said, always hoping the latest man would be the lasting one. Maybe there was still time for children. I didn't need the breaking daylight to show me she was looking at me hopefully. My only hope was that she wouldn't be too disappointed when I left.

She told me a story. During the Second World War her great-grandmother's younger sister had embarked on an affair with a Nazi officer – not for personal gain or status but out of love. I suppose it's the sort of thing that happens when you discover that an occupying army is composed of individuals and not identikit stereotypes, and find that some of them are actually good people trapped by circumstances that make them enemies. When the Germans left Denmark the girl was dragged into the street by a gang of women, beaten, stripped naked and tied to a lamp post with a placard round her neck. It said *hore*. The woman told me the self-righteous bitches had also cut off her great-great-aunt's long, golden hair. Then the woman laughed and said if that's all love is, humiliation and pain, who needs it? Her tone was bitter but it was only a veneer. Beneath it I could hear the desperate hope that what she was saying was a lie. I asked, more to make conversation than out of any real interest, what the victim's name had been. Sif, she told me, named after Thor's mythical wife because she had been born with golden hair down to her shoulders. She said Sif had been the goddess of corn.

I liked her. She was pretty and nice and part of me wishes I could have stayed, like she wanted me to, as she'd asked when I was eating the simple breakfast she made me, coffee and slices of light rye bread with butter and cheese. But I'm not that man she dreams of meeting one day, the lasting one, the wish made flesh. My wish for her is that she doesn't grow old alone. But I have to confess that while I was in her bed I was afraid I might turn to find someone else there instead of her – maybe a cold, leathery cadaver like the Huldremose woman, or perhaps someone still living and whose coldness was on the inside. I have no desire to wake up in the night next to corpses, living or dead. All I want to do is forget and I will continue to try, though I know I never shall.

I wonder what her name was. I never asked.

The train is too hot, a glazed metal trap for the sun's rays. I'm sweating and shivering but I don't know if it's down to last night's beer intake or if I might be going down with flu or something. I showered before I left the woman's apartment but my clothes smell stale, smoky and vaguely beery. The fresh sweat won't make things much worse. The train sways and rattles as it rumbles along the track, which I picture as a yellow ribbon winding among Copenhagen's streets and buildings. A man and woman sit opposite me. The man lights a cigarette, disregarding the signs commanding passengers to desist from smoking. I don't protest. Instead I follow suit. He nods and smiles. I do the same. He crosses his legs and so do I. When I yawn, so does he. He draws on his cigarette and I do likewise. Then I notice he is dressed almost identically to me – in fact, the only differences are that I am wearing a wristwatch while he is not, and he has black boots instead of trainers. I'm momentarily disconcerted, unsure if I'm looking into a mirror that reflects another man's face or perhaps have inadvertently joined in some floating game of Simon Says. The woman is predictably blonde.

Suddenly the mirroring becomes total and I see myself sitting in the seat opposite, and though the woman is still blonde she now has a different face. The train is another train in another country; it is another day, one I remember clearly. They are holding hands and laughing, talking and looking at each other as lovers do when they believe they will always be together. She kisses him and I feel the cold, hard lips of the Huldremose woman pressing against my cheek, those hands like shrivelled leather gauntlets roughly grasping my fingers.

With that all the things I have been drinking to forget flood back and scream a version of the truth that is so beautiful it makes me want to shriek with pain. But it's a lie. A loud buzzing fills my head and in my mind's eye I see the flash of yellow that warns of toxicity and venom, the colour of high-visibility jackets, hazards and dangerous machinery, the hue of the quarantine flag. I want to warn him to get out while he can, to forget the possibilities he sees in the line of her face and the soft blue of her eyes – to escape before he falls completely. Whatever she feels now, no matter what she says today and might even mean, she'll be the death of the man you are, I want to tell him, she will slay you with a single word and you'll become a ghost like me, a spectral drifter who has no substance even in his own mind, a thin creature who wants to write her out of his life but can't find the words to do it. You will become me, because you were me.

It's too late for him, I know that. So I close my eyes tightly and take a dozen deep, slow, shuddering breaths. When I open them the couple are as they were before I slipped into that vision of the past. The train is pulling into a station and I rise from my seat and get out, reeling and stumbling as though I am as drunk as I was last night but not caring what they or anyone else might think of the state I am in. I can't see any signs with the station's name, but where I am doesn't matter because anywhere is better than where I have just been.

On the platform I dizzily light another cigarette, trying to calm myself with that simple mechanical action. But first my trembling fingers are unable to manipulate the lighter then my lungs seem unable to suck in either air or smoke. Above me the late morning sky is too big and too blue, and it turns like a wheel, much too slowly and much too fast.

The sun is too yellow and it won't let me forget.

The Other Side of the River

Two coins fell into the waxed cardboard cup, startling the old man from a painstakingly crafted reconstruction of a sunny afternoon from his barely-remembered youth.

It was a shame, really. He'd finally got to the good bit, where he was sitting on the riverbank with Moira Brennan, a half-empty bottle of wine by his side, his hand inside her blouse, and his free hand poised, waiting for the command to proceed in a more southerly direction. That had been a fine afternoon and Moira had been a splendid young woman, large-breasted and mouthwateringly-arsed. His hand had indeed headed south, to be followed not long after by another part of his anatomy. God, she'd screamed like a banshee on heat when she came. He'd been terrified someone might hear and think she was being murdered but, unable to stop himself, he'd simply carried on until he was screaming just as loudly.

How long ago had that been? Well, it depended on what this year was and he was buggered if he could say. It had happened in 1969, what felt like several lifetimes ago. He'd been nineteen years old. What year was it now? The last date he recalled with any clarity was the May of 1997 when the bloody Tories had been kicked out of Downing Street at last, and he thought at least three winters had come and gone since then; though it could be as many as six or even eight. It was the drink, of course. It was always the drink.

A thought struck him and he opened his grimy raincoat, peeling away a few pages of the newspapers he used for insulation and peering dully at the date. The *Daily Express*, he noted with a degree of satisfaction, Wednesday the 17th of July 2013. Lagging was just about all that Tory rag was good for. Nowadays the newsprint was too shiny too wipe your arse with. But how had it suddenly become 2013? Had the Tories really been gone for sixteen years? No, he realised, after reading a few paragraphs of the smeared front page, the Tories were back and the Lib Dems were now their pet dogs. When had that happened? How had he failed to notice? And was he really sixty-three?

Moira Brennan had left him for an office clerk a year after that golden afternoon. It had broken his heart. A few months later he took his guitar, packed a bag and hitch-hiked north to London, to ease his pain and make his fortune. He'd done alright for a while, gigging in the folk clubs in the city and Home Counties, earning enough to rent a bed-sit, eat and buy a few drinks of an evening, some dope for the weekend. There had been a handful of good reviews in the music press, even some interest from a couple of record labels. Then the gigs dried up, the dole queue beckoned, and all too soon the few drinks became many and the dope was only a hazy memory. He sold his guitar, was kicked out of his home and took to the road, thumbing a lift when his wits were about him, walking when they'd gone for a holiday. He'd done a lot of walking.

One day he'd ended up back in London. Since then it had been nights in parks, shop doorways and alleys; or a hostel when it was too cold or wet and cardboard boxes were scarce. He recalled the occasional run-in with fellow vagrants and a few beatings at the hands of teenagers who had no-one else to hit out at, but those violent encounters were thankfully rare. He wasn't a man for confrontation or fisticuffs. All he wanted to do was sit on a bench in a quiet place and drink himself away. He had a routine: spend the mornings begging and spend the money he made on cheap booze. It worked just fine, most of the time.

He called to the disappearing back of his latest benefactor. 'Thanks, mate! God bless!'

Not that God had ever blessed anyone he knew of, except maybe that spotty office boy who'd taken his Moira away.

Not a bad morning's takings. Nearly ten quid had fallen from generous hands into his cardboard cup. Now it was evening. He sat on a bench on the Embankment near Cleopatra's Needle, looking south across the river. A bottle of Thunderbird, concealed in a brown paper bag, was already open and a third empty; another bottle nestled in his overcoat pocket, next to his remaining coins. It was going to be a fine night – the afternoon heat lingered, the sky was clear and the wind was as gentle as an angel's gasp. There were tourists, clocked-off shop and office workers milling around, and he felt perfectly safe.

So he was sixty-three. Who'd have thought it? He'd

never expected to live this long. Sure, he was a drunk and a tramp and suffered the usual ailments that could be expected from self-neglect and long exposure to the elements, but he wasn't in bad shape, all things considered. In fact, this evening he was feeling unusually well. He wasn't too surprised to be in such good mental and physical form, though. Thinking about Moira always bucked him up, made his pulse quicker and the blood warmer.

That afternoon by the river had been one of many such beautiful times they'd shared. He and Moira had been an item for nearly three years, all but inseparable for most of the last two. Their friends and family expected it to go all the way – marriage, mortgage, kids and a car. Except that he had plans that didn't lead in their direction, at least not entirely. The songs and performances called more strongly than they did. But while playing in the clubs and pubs brought in enough to keep himself, it would never be enough to keep both of them. And just when he realised that he would be forced to choose between two conflicting dreams, Moira left him for that guy whose name he could no longer remember – that he didn't *want* to remember.

The second bottle was going down as nicely as the first. The sun was going down too, the western skyline bathed in shades of red and orange. His vision was slightly blurred, which was understandable as he was more than slightly drunk.

He wondered where Moira was now, what she was doing. Was she still with the nameless clerk? Was she happy? Did she have children and grandchildren to light up her twilight years? Was she well?

Suddenly the weight of the coins in his left coat pocket

seemed to pull him down on that side. He almost had to fight to stay sitting upright on the bench. Something had to be done about that. He put his hand in his pocket, rummaged around and eventually brought out two tenpence pieces. Immediately, his balance returned to normal. But was that all he had? He could have sworn he had more than that. It had certainly felt like many more coins. He gazed drunkenly at the pavement around the bench but could see nothing except a lot of cigarette ends, a couple of empty crisp packets and a scrawny pigeon shuffling around hopefully on one leg, the other terminating in a blunt stump just below the knee. He pitied the pigeon but laughed at his own thought. Did birds have knees? And did that matter to anyone but the birds?

That brought Moira to mind again. One of her quirks, one of the things he'd loved about her, was her tendency to refer to animals' bodies in human terms. The front legs of a cat or dog were 'arms' and a horse's hooves were 'feet'. A bird didn't have a beak but a mouth. Her terminology wasn't the product of ignorance or stupidity, he'd quickly realised – Moira was a bright, well-read girl – but was born from fellow-feeling, an acceptance that other creatures were people and deserved to be spoken of in the same way.

He placed the empty second bottle with its twin on the pavement by the bench. They would go in the bin when he decided to leave. He wished he had a third because he didn't want to think about Moira anymore.

'Are you OK?' She was a young woman, maybe thirty years old. His eyes widened as he looked up at her. Her eyes were green and she seemed concerned. He was shocked. If it hadn't been for the hair, dark brown instead of the chestnut he expected, she could have been Moira's double. She even held herself the same way. For a moment he thought he would faint.

'Yes – yes, thank you. I'm fine, just a bit tired.' *And more than a bit pissed*, he almost added, but thought better of it. The he felt ashamed, because his voice came out as a hoarse croak, the timbre he had always so detested in those hopeless alcoholics he'd always looked down on. *And that's what I am now*, he finally admitted. *That's what I am now*. He wanted her to go away, to leave him alone with his humiliation. He wanted her to go away because he couldn't stand the thought of her looking at him.

She smiled uncertainly, clearly not swayed by his claim to be simply tired. She opened her mouth as if to say something, but was interrupted.

'Sally! Come on, we can walk across the bridge to the station. The train leaves in an hour so we can get a coffee first.'

Looking past the woman called Sally, he saw them – a woman about the same age as himself, still slim but with a lot of grey in her red hair, in a floral print dress. Beside her stood a stooped, bald man in a suit and fashionable spectacles at least four decades too young for him. They were laden with bags – Monsoon, Harrods, House of Fraser. Nothing cheap. These were people who'd done well for themselves.

The young woman smiled once more and dug into a purse. 'Here,' she said, pressing something into his hand. 'Buy yourself a good meal. No drink. Promise?'

He merely nodded. She smiled once more and left. He watched as she joined her parents and he continued watching as they mounted the stairs to the bridge, following them with his eyes until they reached the other side and were lost in the crowds milling around the Royal Festival Hall. Then he unclenched his hand and saw that he was now the proud owner of a twenty-pound note.

She hadn't recognised him. Of course she hadn't. How could she? His beard was as long, grey and tangled as his hair. His face was lined and scarred, the skin grimy and rough, laced with broken capillaries. He was a shadow of the man he'd once been, a distorted reflection in a dirty, broken mirror. His heart ached at his anonymity in her sight. But he was glad she hadn't known who he was.

And now he knew what had become of her.

He leaned back and closed his eyes and impulsively laid the two coins on his eyelids. The metal discs were cool and soothing. He became drowsy.

The man was in the same pose two hours later when a policeman tried to move him on. By then the banknote had gone, and so had the coins. They were probably already fuelling another homeless person's bid for amnesia. Something else had gone too, following a lost dream to the other side of the river.

Post-It

Session One

There was another message for me this morning. Like the others it was written in black ballpoint on a yellow Post-It note, three words by an anonymous hand in block capitals. This one was stuck on the wall above the toilet bowl, at my eye level so I couldn't miss it when taking my first leak of the day.

TAKE THE BUS

I stuck the note on the sugar bowl and subjected it to abstracted scrutiny while I ate my toast, drank coffee and smoked a couple of cigarettes. This was the fifth note I had discovered in the space of two weeks. Its precursors had been just as brief, equally cryptic. All had been placed with uncanny precision, as though whoever was responsible had access not only to my daily timetable but also to any deviations from it.

The first note had been placed on my wardrobe door. That day I had an interview for a job and had spent much of the previous evening worrying about what I should wear, Normally, I dress casually – it's that kind of employer – but obviously I ought to wear a suit for an interview. I'd decided on a navy blue shirt but couldn't settle on a tie. Should I go for something sombre or choose one that was colourful but restrained and showed that I was a fun-loving but capable bloke who would enhance both morale and business? The note was to the point.

BLACK TIE TODAY

I thought about it for a few minutes then reached into the wardrobe and took out a black silk tie with a faint embossed pattern. I figured I had nothing to lose. At the interview I saw that each one of the panel was wearing black suits with black ties. Everyone seemed subdued and I had noticed that one of the receptionists had obviously been weeping. I was informed that everyone in the firm was upset because a popular manager had died suddenly the previous day, the victim of a mugging that had gone spectacularly bad only a few yards from the office. The interview was sombre and formal, with none of the usual sanity-testing left-field questions potential employers often use to catch candidates out. And they seemed to approve of my sober demeanour, which fitted perfectly with the ambience. The next day I had a telephone call telling me I'd been the outstanding candidate and the job was mine if I wanted it. Naturally, I accepted.

The following evening, as I was sitting at my home computer checking my e-mails, my cigarette lighter ran out of gas. I put a hand into the desk compartment where I keep my smoking accoutrements and fumbled for a spare lighter. My hand encountered something unfamiliar and I found that someone had stuck another note on one of my lighters. The message was once again short and sweet.

TOMORROW CALL IN SICK

The next morning I did just that. Gerry, my boss, sounded a bit sceptical when I told him I was feeling unwell and I'm not sure my list of conflicting symptoms did much to convince him, but what the hell – I'd already landed a better job with a higher salary.

At around three that afternoon, as I was in my flat lying on the sofa with a good book, a pot of tea and a plate of chocolate Hobnobs, the local radio station interrupted its golden oldies programme to give details of a robbery at the computer shop where I worked. A couple of thugs had gone in with guns, emptied the till and stuffed a hold-all with iPods and mobile phones, then shot every member of staff: Gerry had been killed outright, while Jennie and Frank had both been badly wounded.

As you can imagine, I was stunned. It began to sink in that someone, somewhere, working in very mysterious ways, was looking out for me. I phoned the police station, told them who I was and was horrified to discover that since the newsflash had been broadcast Jennie had died and Frank's condition had deteriorated. A couple of detectives came round to interview me – there wasn't much I could tell them and for while it seemed I might be under suspicion, but as they were giving me the third degree they took a call to say the killers had been apprehended, apparently while trying to sell the stolen gear to an off-duty constable who had been shopping at a street market just across the road from the nick. No wonder they'd turned to a life of crime – they were obviously far too thick to hold down a normal job.

The next day dawned dully and depressingly. OK, I

was still alive and had a new job to replace the one I clearly couldn't go to anymore. I was sad at my colleagues' deaths and wounding, but realised that there was another pressing issue. It was Gerry's shop and he sorted out all the pay. Until all the police procedures were concluded and the legal stuff was worked out I had no income. I wasn't due to start my new job for another few weeks. Even if I signed on it would be at least four weeks before I was paid. All I had was a twenty pound note and a fistful of change. My head began to ache.

When I opened the bathroom cabinet to get some painkillers I found another Post-It on the box of paracetemol.

PELICAN BAY BABY
SANGRIA NIGHTS

My unknown benefactor was either getting into anagrams or feeling very whimsical and cryptic indeed. I ate my breakfast in my usual leisurely way, smoked a couple of roll-ups and did some housework. Then I made some tea and settled back on the sofa with my interrupted book. Suddenly, I sat bolt upright: I thought I knew what this message meant. I grabbed my keys and that last twenty quid and hurried round the corner to the betting shop. Sure enough, Pelican Bay Baby was running in the 4.15 at Lingfield, while Sangria Nights was in the 4.45. They were both outsiders. The last two races of the day, and the time was 4.05. I put the entire twenty on Pelican Bay Baby to win and kept my fingers crossed. When that horse came in at 12-1 I nearly passed out. When the bookie handed me my £260 I didn't even hesitate. The whole lot went on Sangria Nights, which proceeded to romp home at 10-1.

Walking home with nearly three grand in my pocket made me feel a whole lot better. The bookie's venomous glare worried me not one bit. I called in at the chippie for a celebratory pie and chips, with a gherkin and a can of Pepsi for that touch of decadence. But there was still something of a gloomy cloud hanging over me. When I got home I rang Interflora and had flowers sent to Gerry's wife and Jennie's girlfriend, with another bouquet to Frank in the hospital. But I knew it wouldn't make any of them feel better and it didn't assuage my survivor guilt.

A few more days when by and then message number four arrived. It was on the television screen when I went to switch on for *Match of the Day*. I was certain it hadn't been there a couple of minutes earlier.

STAY HOME TOMORROW

That was annoying. I had planned to take a train to Brighton to visit my family and maybe spend some time in my old local with whatever old friends might turn up on the night. Still, my mysterious benefactor had done well by me so far. Reluctantly, I phoned my folks to tell them I couldn't make it.

The next day three things happened. Firstly, while I was pottering about in the kitchen making breakfast I noticed smoke coming from the back of the microwave. I unplugged the machine straight away, grateful that I had probably averted a fire. I briefly considered perhaps going to Brighton after all, but reflected that the note hadn't told me to have a late breakfast or take a later train – it had specifically instructed me to stay at home. I decided to stay.

Just after noon, I heard noises at my back door. Looking out of a side window I saw that some young villain in a hooded top was trying to break into my home' He was having some difficulty with the lock so I figured it would be safe to leave him at it for a little while longer. I used my mobile phone to call the police, suggesting that it might be a good idea not to use sirens, so they could catch him in the act. I sat back and waited. The police arrived pretty quickly and grabbed him without too much trouble. When the police had cuffed him and pulled down his hood I almost felt sorry for him. He was a skinny young black kid, maybe fifteen or sixteen years old, with a trapped, haunted look on his face. He didn't look at all well and I thought maybe he was a junkie who had been after something to sell to pay for his next fix. My sympathy lasted only until the copper in charge pulled a nasty-looking knife from the kid's hold-all and I imagined what that could have done to my delicate flesh. When the police had taken my statement, made sure they got the boy's fingerprints from the door and gone, I made some coffee and listened to a couple of CDs.

In the evening I tuned my television to the BBC News channel and was astonished to learn that there had been a series of power failures affecting most of the rail network south of London. The train I had been due to take had been stalled between stations about halfway to Brighton. The electricity supply still hadn't been fixed and the newsreader was talking about thousands of passengers stranded across the region, with many having to spend the night on trains because there wasn't any way to move them.

Session Two
It is now evening. I did indeed take the bus to my new job. Inevitably the bus was stuck in traffic and about a mile

from my new place of employment the bus stopped and we were all ordered out, no reasons given. I decided to walk the rest of the way, slightly alarmed to hear and see a lot of emergency service vehicle hurtling through the streets. I was late but that became a small detail, forgotten and forgiven almost immediately, and my apologies were waved away. This was because I was one of the few people to make it in. While I was sitting on the bus, in a horrific echo of 7/7 a series of bombs had exploded across the Tube network and in a couple of the mainline terminus stations: Kings Cross, Victoria, Euston, London Bridge, Bank, Charing Cross, Waterloo, Oxford Circus, Liverpool Street, Fenchurch Street, Tottenham Court Road (my intended destination), Paddington – I lost count as we crowded round the television and gazed in horror at the emerging carnage. Hundreds had been killed and the death-toll was climbing all the time. A reporter spoke of rumours that a vast fire was raging out of control beneath the streets of central London.

We had no customers and none of us had the heart to work. The manager went out and came back with whisky and vodka. After phoning the head office he closed the shop. None of the missing staff phoned in. Those few of us that had made it drank and talked quietly. At around three o'clock the manager told us we should try to get home. I faced a long and tortuous journey home – virtually the entire West End was impassable as the emergency services tried desperately to rescue people, treat survivors and fight the fires. All the bridges across the Thames were closed. There were no buses running and the Tube was quite clearly totally screwed. The manager was kind enough to drive me to the Greenwich foot tunnel, and I managed to get a cab at the southern end.

I didn't know whether to laugh or cry. That message had almost certainly saved my life. But why couldn't the author have given me more information so I could at least have tried to save others, even running the risk of being suspected of involvement in that terrible crime? I was distraught at the suffering and loss of life, and my survivor guilt was up and running again. For some reason I felt almost personally responsible for it all, though quite clearly it was nothing whatsoever to do with me. I couldn't shake off an intense and inexplicable sense of remorse. It was a cruel salvation.

Up to now I haven't really thought about who was sending the messages or how they knew what was going to happen. You may find that surprising – and so do I. I'm a naturally inquisitive – not to mention innately sceptical – person and with hindsight it was astonishing that I hadn't even questioned the notes but had just gone along with every single one. Sure, I had considered not complying – but it was a token gesture. I had known every time that I would obey. Somehow, for some reason I am unable to explain, I trust the sender.

But this latest obscene brutality has shaken me out of that complacent trance. Right now, I'm frightened and confused. Who knows my life so well that they can manipulate me this way? And why should they only manipulate me for my own benefit? Why didn't they use their foreknowledge to save lives? Who apart from me is gaining from this? And, the biggest question of all: how can they know what my future holds?

I've had a fair bit to drink now and I'm more than slightly pissed. I was going to stay up late to watch the Perseid meteor shower but I'm too damned tired and too damned distressed and I'm going to bed. Maybe I can sleep.

Session Three
It's two-thirty in the morning and somehow I'm wide awake. I'm standing naked by the front door with no memory of how I got here. My heart is pounding and I'm drenched in my own sweat, hyperventilating and shaking. In my hands is a standard-size yellow Post-It note. There is a message on it, block capitals in black ink.

GET OUT NOW

Confused and frightened, I hesitate. I can hear a rushing sound like a high wind and a crackling sound like someone's crushing a slice of burnt toast. Moving at last, I try to open the door but the security chain is on. In my panic, I push the latch on as I fumble to remove the chain with hands that refuse to obey my commands. Eventually I manage to get the door unlocked, unchained and open. I take one step through it.

***Déjà Vu* all over again**
As you have probably deduced, I didn't write the preceding sections. It's actually an edited transcript of tape recordings made while I was undergoing hypnotic regression ten years ago. There's nothing after that until I was found, semi-conscious, lacerated and pretty scorched, in a hospital car park. For a time, I had no memory of my past. It was only when I began to recover from the physical trauma that I began to remember my life, though the events recounted

above continued to elude me until that breakthrough hypnotherapy session.

Officially, however, I remained a John Doe. As far as the authorities are concerned, I have total amnesia – I have language, basic life skills and general knowledge, but no life, no identity. That's the official version. For a long time, the police were suspicious of me. After ruling out any connection between my injuries and criminal activity, and confirming that I had no DNA or fingerprints on file, they concluded that I probably wasn't either a known felon or a suspect. They then assumed that I was an illegal immigrant of some sort. But a battery of tests revealed that, personal information apart, I knew an awful lot about British history, the nation's geography, sport and culture; and that I spoke English like the native I am. At my own insistence they drilled out a section of tooth and tests on that confirmed that I had spent almost my entire life on these shores. Social workers and a solicitor arranged for me to be given a temporary identity, a national insurance number, and a place in a hostel. I had to report to a police station once a month but was otherwise free to build something resembling a normal life. I got a job in a factory then spent a few years making something of myself once again.

The reason for my subterfuge is simple enough. When I was in that hospital I happened to catch sight of a newspaper that one of the other patients was reading. The front page headline announced that the previous day's General Election had been won by Labour, led by Tony Blair. Despite my shock, I kept quiet. Something was clearly very wrong. The Blair victory had happened in 1997. But my last, incomplete, memories were of events that took place late in the summer of 2017.

The next day's newspapers continued the post-election coverage. People in the ward were talking about it. Somehow I had escaped some devastating incident only to been transported back in time. I realised that something truly astonishing had taken place but I couldn't talk about it. No one would believe me and I'd probably end up locked away in a psychiatric unit. Although things were looking pretty weird I wasn't too distraught about this bombshell. I'd just stay put, be careful about what I said, and see what happened.

It gradually dawned on me that I had an opportunity to live a very different kind of life. I knew the outcome of some major sporting and political events, the way the housing market would develop, and which companies were worth investment. If I played my cards right I could make a lot of money and keep it safe; and there was a lot I could do with that wealth, though I'd have to be careful about influencing world events the wrong way. I'd read enough science fiction to know that altering the past was not a good idea. I've made a particular, focused effort to learn more about quantum physics, and have used my new financial leverage to consult some of the greatest minds in the field. So far I've managed to amass a lot of theories but no answers. My best guess is that my home was struck by a meteor, or something that coincided with the meteor shower that night, and the impact triggered some sort of quantum event that propelled me back into the past. The how and why of it are matters of conjecture. I suppose it doesn't matter – I'm here, now, and have made the most of it. I've had the unique opportunity to live through a period of history twice, and in the process I've found everything I ever wanted and more, except for a solution to the central conundrum of my existence.

So here I am, very nearly twenty years later but at the same point in time. I'm a very rich man indeed, but in a quiet way that attracts little attention. I have new friends, a family, a beautiful home, and the freedom to pursue all those interests I never had much time for in my old life. In many respects I'm living out my own fantasy. The hypnotic regression – God knows what the therapist made of it – showed me what needed to be done to ensure that everything turned out this way. Yes, I have moral qualms – in a way, all those deaths that are to come, and which I have already seen, will be on my conscience. I could prevent them but I must not, for the sake of history. Or so I tell myself. I tell myself that I must keep events on track, not for my own benefit but because they are already written into the fabric of time. Sometimes I even believe myself.

Right now, I'm sitting in my car outside the flat where I used to live. It is just after midnight. I have a key to the door, obtained by a private detective, and a pad of yellow Post-It notes. On the top note I have written a brief message, in as anonymous a hand as I could manage. It looks more or less as I remember it.

BLACK TIE TODAY

I have an hour or so to wait until I'm asleep. Then I will creep into the flat and affix the note to my wardrobe door, taking great care not to wake myself up. It will be an emotional moment but I shall resist the temptation to wallow in nostalgia. I won't wander around the flat looking at my old stuff, touching this or that once-treasured item.

Sentimentality is not on the agenda. I'll be in and out as quickly as I can. I need to be very careful to change nothing, to keep history on its set course. After all, it's not often one gets the chance to save one's own life twenty years after the fact. Not that it actually is, but you know what I mean.

It's also quite exciting in another way. In a few weeks from now, for the first time in twenty years, I won't know what the future holds for me or for anyone else. I look forward to that. In real terms I'm only forty-five now and it will be a great relief not to spend another thirty years or so watching politicians, pop stars, footballers and ersatz celebrities making their bad decisions for the second time. The uncertainty is exhilarating.

In the Beginning was the Word

The Lord looked upon his creation and was dissatisfied. The divine brow was furrowed and the celestial countenance was grim. He had moved upon the face of the waters, uttered the magic word and gazed lovingly at his new world. The plants had been fun to put together, as had the animals – but then the Lord had grown tired and bored. He realised that he only actually knew one word, and that had now been used up. What was he going to call all those great things he'd made? How could he call them anything when he didn't have any more words? He didn't even have a name for himself. Then that single word he did know came in handy when the bulb lit up above his head. If he couldn't name his new toys he would make something else, a creature that would have so many words that he could name everything and still have plenty left over for anything else the Lord might turn his omnipotent hand to. Maybe he would learn some new words from this latest idea.

So he took a spare ape, made some minor adjustments and so produced a talking animal, a male who played the game and gave names to everything he laid eyes on. The Almighty was well pleased. *So that funny-looking thing was called an elephant? Wow – great name! And that monstrosity was a rhinoceros? That really cool one is a tiger? Excellent! And so many different beetles – only meant to create a few thousand types for specific jobs, must have lost count. But for the life of me I can't remember why I made the koala – must have thought it was cute.* The Lord learned an awful lot of words in those first few days with his pet chatterbox. Most of the words didn't seem to mean much but the Lord could live with that.

After a while the talkative animal – who called himself Man – twigged that something wasn't quite right. He loudly and at great length pointed out to the Lord that all the animals came in pairs. One half of each pair was equipped in a way similar to Man, with things that were clearly designed to fit neatly into a place on the other half of each pair. This equipment appeared to be both practical – part of the process the Lord had dreamed up whereby his creatures could make more of themselves – and recreational. Man wasn't all that interested in replicating himself but he wanted in on the recreational aspect. He told the Lord in no uncertain terms that this was bloody unfair. The Lord slapped his omniscient forehead with the palm of an omnipotent hand and shame-facedly admitted to Man that he'd screwed up. So to keep the peace he made something very much like Man, only equipped differently, and heaved a sigh of relief when Man looked upon the Lord's latest creation and was pleased. Man called the newcomer Woman. She was just as chatty as Man, if not more so.

And that's when the trouble began, because it meant that Man and Woman made many more of themselves and soon the whole of creation was overrun with chattering, yapping, gossiping, complaining windbags who couldn't shut up if they wanted to. After a few thousand years the Lord had heard enough. He packed his bags and left for a different space-time continuum where he could begin all over again. This time he would know lots and lots of words and could name everything he made without having to rely on an under-dressed chimpanzee that had far too many words to express the few worthwhile thoughts in its brain.

Left to their own devices, Man and Woman eventually decided that one language was nowhere near enough to fill their needs, so they made their offspring spread across the entire planet just so they could make more languages. They reasoned that if left in isolation their descendants would begin to speak differently from one another. They were right on the money. After a while, Man and Woman – who by this time had invented a lot of new names for their kind, including 'humans' – had thousands of new languages in which to indulge their main pastime, namely idle chit-chat.

But even that wasn't enough. Humans at large were as arrogant and conceited as they were loquacious. Every single man and woman believed that their incoherent rants and inane ramblings were so important that they should be preserved, never to be forgotten. A few bright sparks invented writing – learning to do it was hard work that cut down on available yapping time, so it took several attempts and a couple of thousand years before the written word finally caught on. Pretty soon though, every last piece of empty-headed nonsense they spoke found its way into one or other of the written forms they had devised. Yes, even one kind of writing wasn't enough for them.

Making signs on clay tablets or sheets of papyrus or slabs of stone didn't satisfy them either. It was a slow process and besides, it meant that only a few people at a time would have access to their precious, cosmically significant words. Now humans, inherently lazy animals, had invented all kinds of machines to help them in their labours – the surprisingly unspoken goal was to make a machine that would do everything for them while they lazed around talking pointless crap all day – and it wasn't too long before someone had invented the printing press. This caused a buzz of excitement as humans realised that they could actually mechanise idle gossip. Within a few hundred years humans had printed books and newspapers, and devised several methods of dispersing their conversations in textual format, beginning with the postal system, which quickly developed into the telegraph, radio and television, the telephone, answering machines, and e-mail. E-mail led inexorably to Facebook and Twitter, which many saw as the last word – well, the last few billion words – in mindless nattering.

But humans' greatest achievement, the thing they saw as their crowning glory and their *raison d'être* made manifest, was without question the mobile phone. That one took on a life of its own. Text messaging! Voicemail! Every last word delivered to a captive audience! Talk to anyone, anywhere, anytime! It was a human dream cast in plastic and bits of metal. Within ten years of its invention, the mobile phone was *de rigueur* for humans, many of whom could soon barely function without one. People that opted out of the mobile phone club were sneered at, made fun of, and generally treated like the pariahs they clearly were, until they toed the line, knuckled down and put their shoulders to the wheel, bravely putting their best foot forward and keeping a straight face and stiff upper lip. Conformity, even to the noblest ideals, is tough on the body.

One day, the Lord decided to drop in on his once-favourite creation (he had long ago come to prefer the blessedly quiet aardvark; and in his new home the dominant life-form among was the sweet-natured, playful Noname, which the Lord had been careful to design without either vocal chords or the hard-wiring necessary for language development) to see what kind of unholy cock-ups the silly, noisy buggers had made in his absence. He materialised in the public library in Peckham and spent a couple of minutes reading the *Encyclopaedia Britannica* from cover to cover. (In his exile the Lord had become a bit rusty at omniscience but he'd become an excellent speed reader.) It was a 1990s edition and well out of date, but the Lord quickly got the message. Humans had made a complete dog's breakfast of everything they did. Most of it, inevitably, was related to words. Major wars and had been waged and horrible atrocities committed over the words in two books that purported to be about or even dictated by the Lord himself, though he was pretty damned sure he'd never uttered a single one of the words attributed to him, except the one in the first chapter of the older of the two volumes. The words in one of those books also said that the Lord had a son, though he was quite certain he'd cut his losses and departed for that alternative universe many millennia before the child was even conceived.

In truth, what humans had done to the world, their

animal brethren and each other was appalling. And most of their vicious follies were caused by words. What kind of lunatic would fight to the death over what was written in a book? What kind of creature would invent words that hurt others of its kind? The Lord looked around the library, read a few hundred more books and shook his numinous head in disbelief. He couldn't believe that even humans would read some of this crap. And it went on and on, millions and millions of books; and barely a shred of truth between them.

Downhearted, the Lord decided to go for a walk to see if there were any ducks around. The Lord really liked ducks and – remembering what he'd read in those books – hoped that the humans hadn't excommunicated, executed, tortured, enslaved or eaten every last one of them. He wished himself over to the lake at Greenwich Park and was rewarded with the sight of several mallards and a few species he didn't recognise. That's evolution for you, he thought, always a few surprises, some pleasant. More ducks was always good. He made a few clucking sounds and the ducks swam or waddled to where he sat on a bench with a loaf of bread he'd absent-mindedly conjured from somewhere. He was glad to hear their happy quacks. They made so much more sense than human speech. Pretty soon the ducks had been joined by dozens of other birds, along with a small army of squirrels and little rodents. They recognised their Creator and were pleased to see him, even if the humans didn't give a monkey's.

After a while the Lord decided to return to his new home. He thought it might be a good idea to walk. It was only a few trillion miles and a quick transdimensional shift, and he could use some exercise. As he was strolling through the park he caught sight of a young human male holding a small, rectangular object to his ear and apparently talking to it. The man finished his conversation – the usual meaningless drivel, delivered with barely a pause to draw breath – and began fiddling with small buttons on the device's surface. Intrigued, the Lord activated his telescopic vision and zoomed in. It was fascinating, a small mobile gadget that could be used for verbal communication and which could send and receive short texts or longer e-mails – a tiny machine that could surf the internet and be used to catch up with the latest news. It had maps, games, GPS, music, a clock, a built-in camera, and many other useful things. It was called a *smartphone*.

'Wow,' said the Lord in an idiom he had only recently learned, 'that is seriously cool. I really must get one of those.'

Touching the Zero

Ice sketched fractured flowers on the window and dangled in inverted spires from the eaves. It was too cold for snow, as her mother liked to say; but there was snow anyway, several inches deep in the open and swept into drifts wherever there was a wall. In the garden the skeletal trees had become delicate white lace sculptures haunted by the memory of birds and squirrels. The world had that spectral glow snow always brings, when its albedo triumphs over the woolly grey clouds that gave it birth.

A blackbird had left a message in cuneiform on the patio snowscape. Emma couldn't decipher it. More snow was falling. She hoped the bird had found food and a relatively warm place to shelter.

It was too warm indoors but she couldn't feel it.

Cold hands, warm heart. That was another of her mother's sayings. That wasn't true either, no matter how well-meant. Despite the central heating her hands were chilled and her heart was as cold as the space between stars, as cold as it was possible to be. This shouldn't be what Christmas is like, she thought. It should be blazing fires, cheeks flushed rosy with cheerful drinks, good company and generous meals. It should be presents and laughter, games and stories that gave you goosebumps and made you so glad you were surrounded by people who loved you and would never let you come to harm.

White Christmases weren't often seen in these parts – rare as hen's teeth, according to Mum – but she wasn't sure this one should be welcomed. Grief should be black and wet, all darkness and tears. Wasn't that what her life was at that moment? The pain of loss, the absence of vision, the constant weeping for what could never be brought back, that was what she had. It felt like that was all she had.

At least they had the generous meal to almost look forward to. Her mother was busy in the kitchen, putting the turkey that was far too big for two into a slow oven. For the moment she could smell the freshly made sage and onion stuffing but that would soon be displaced by the aroma of cooking poultry. She doubted that it would make her mouth water as it had done so often in the past. How could she eat a turkey that had been carved by someone other than her father?

'Emma?' The voice betrayed a forced jollity. Her mother was being brave, carrying on with Christmas as though nothing had changed. She was trying to pretend everything was fine, for both their sakes. But it wasn't, not with Dad only three weeks in his grave; not with him gone.

A freak accident, they'd said. High winds, heavy rain and a big roadside tree falling on his car as he'd been driving home from a Saturday afternoon visit to one of his old friends. One of those things no one could predict and nothing could have prevented except improbable foresight. He'd lived long enough for the ambulance to get him to hospital but not long enough for them to get there to say goodbye. He'd suffered multiple serious fractures, massive brain damage, thoracic and abdominal trauma, and significant blood loss. The medics probably hadn't known where to start. If he'd been driving slightly slower or a little bit faster he would have been safe; a second either way, the solemn policeman had suggested. One second.

Emma stirred from the window and went into the kitchen to help her mother. She peeled and sliced potatoes, switched on the deep fryer, opened a can of beans and poured them into a pan. She buttered bread, and prepared a frying pan. This had been their customary Christmas Eve main meal – fried eggs, chips and beans, something simple before the following day's feast. Emma had always liked cooking but this seemed pointless and almost sacrilegious. She did it anyway, even though she knew she would only pick at her food and most of it would be put out for the birds and foxes.

In the end, Emma and her mother donated around three-quarters of their dinner to the local wildlife. Emma also gave the birds a mince pie, which she crumbled around the left-overs. It was dark by then, and the snow seemed even brighter. With the clouds now gone it shone with the house lights and brightening stars. There were more bird-tracks and some marks that suggested a large cat or small fox. She stood as still as she could for a few minutes but nothing approached. In the distance someone laughed and there was a brief burst of thumping bass noise as someone drove past with their car stereo turned up to maximum. Emma turned her gaze skyward, just in time to see a brief flash, a shooting star. She knew it was only a chunk of icy rock burning away in the atmosphere but she closed her eyes and made a wish anyway. She would never get her Dad back but she wished him a happy Christmas, wherever he was.

She swallowed back the lump that come to her throat and blinked away prickling tears, then walked back down the garden path and into the house. Her mother was watching television, an old black and white film about a man in the depths of despair who was about to kill himself when an angel showed him how bad things would be without him. Mum was crying, but that was nothing new. Sentimental films always did that to her. Emma was just glad they weren't showing *Ghost*. That one always made her mother howl, and this year – well, that would be too much. She made a mental note to check the television guide and make sure it wasn't being broadcast over the holidays. If it was she would break the television or something.

There were fewer presents than usual under the Christmas tree. They were wrapped in shiny red and green paper, and tied with silver ribbon. Emma had only one present for her mother, a hand-carved wooden picture frame from a nearby craft shop. Emma thought it was lovely. It would be nice for a photograph of her Dad. It had cost her several weeks' pocket money. Emma felt slightly guilty about that because she knew her mother was worried about money. They would struggle to pay the mortgage with only one income, at least until Dad's life insurance was sorted out. But if it made her Mum feel better for only five minutes then it would be money well spent.

The film – *It's a Wonderful Life*, Mum said it was called, one of her favourites – ended and they watched the news together, but that was depressing so they switched off. At ten o'clock Emma went to bed. She was eleven and felt more grown-up than she should be since her Dad had died, but she was too tired to stay up and keep her mother company. She got ready for bed, carefully wrapped the picture frame ready for the morning, and was asleep almost as soon as her head touched the pillow.

She dreamed of clocks, their hands spinning backwards and forwards, speeding up and slowing down. There were hundreds of them, thousands – perhaps millions. She walked through corridors lined with them and into rooms that were filled with the things, in all shapes and sizes. After what seemed hours, she came to a room that had only one timepiece, a large grandfather clock with a pendulum that swung erratically, sometimes stopping altogether before starting up again.

'You can't turn back the clock,' said her father. 'Well, you can – but time keeps on going just like it always does. The straight line we live goes on and what happens along the way can't be undone.'

'But I want everything to be the way it was,' she said. 'I want you to come back.'

Dad laughed and gave her a hug. 'You'd better be careful what you say,' he advised her. 'There's a famous story about a woman who wished that her dead son would come back. She had this magic monkey's paw that would grant a wish. And it did, but she hadn't thought it through and when her son returned – well, he was still dead but moving around. Her husband realised what was happening and he wished his son back into his grave before the mother saw him. That would have been a terrible thing to see. You wouldn't that for me, would you? And what about that film your Mum just watched. If everything was to suddenly return to a time just before I died then all the good things that have happened to other people since then might not happen. It would change things, you see? And I might die anyway, but in an even worse way. No, even if you could somehow fix things it probably wouldn't be for the better.'

'But I miss you,' she told him. 'And Mum's so sad. I'm sad too.'

'I know. But you shouldn't change anything even if you could. The way things are is the way they were meant to be. Anyway, I'm here with you now. I'll always be with you, you know that; always in your heart, just as you and your Mum will always be in mine.'

'But you're dead. Your heart doesn't work anymore. How can we be there?'

He sat cross-legged on the polished wooden floor, just like he'd always done when they talked, and she snuggled up next to him. He was wearing his favoured jeans and a checked shirt, and had his usual two or three days' stubble. He needed a haircut. He didn't have any shoes or socks on. That was just like him.

'Being dead is very strange. It isn't at all what I expected. It's not like Heaven or Hell, or anything you read about. It's sort of like being alive but without the need to do anything or be anywhere. I never see anyone else, though I can look in on you and your mother every now and then. There's no sense of time passing. I just exist, and I'm quite content with that. Except that I'm worried about you two, of course. I don't like to see you so sad and afraid for the future.' He pointed at the grandfather clock. 'Do you notice anything unusual about that clock?'

She looked carefully at it but it seemed perfectly ordinary, apart from that crazily unpredictable pendulum. Then she saw it.

'The numbers are wrong. It goes from one to twelve in the right order like any other clock, but then there's a zero. It's right at the top where the twelve should be. Both the hands are touching the zero and they're not moving even though the pendulum is going mad. All the other numbers are...' She groped for the right word.

'Displaced?'

'Yes, that's right. The spaces between them are smaller than they should be, crushed up closer together to make room for the zero. Why is there a zero? You can't have "nought o'clock" or "ten to nought", can you?'

'Not usually, no. Certainly not in your world, the place I used to live. Numbers are funny things. You need a zero to do maths, but what does it actually mean? When you use numbers to measure distance, it's the place you start out from, the beginning. Think about it – that first mark on a ruler or tape measure is zero. Everything else comes after that. But when you measure quantity or volume, you use a zero to mean nothing. It's the absence of something, emptiness. When you do sums the zero indicates that you've come to the end of a quantity of ten, so it completes what you can count the natural way, on the fingers of two hands. So it's a sort of end point, too.'

Emma was quiet for a moment. She knew her father was good at arithmetic but this seemed to go beyond mathematics and into another realm of thought entirely. Zero was where you started, where you ended, and nothing at all. A nought seemed to mean an awful lot.

'Clocks don't start at zero, do they? The hands start at twelve, then they go on to one. And when they get back round to twelve it starts again. It's like recycling, though obviously you can't have the same twelve hours over and over. That would be silly. Nothing would ever get done.'

'That's right,' her Dad replied. 'Measuring time is different again. You can never have "no time". Einstein tells us that time is a dimension of space. If there was no space there would be no time. There would have to be nothing whatsoever, anywhere, for time to run out. It works the other way round, too. No time would mean no space. And space and time go on forever, until they stop.'

Emma's head was beginning to spin. 'Dad, this all getting a bit *Alice in Wonderland* for me. Can't you just tell me why the clock has a zero?'

He laughed again. The sound made her heart warmer and sadder at the same time.

'Emma, where I am now all of time happens at once. It's a place, and I'm always everywhere in it. Right now, I'm watching you being born, and seeing your first day at school, your graduation from university, your wedding, your children, and your funeral. Everywhere in space and time is the place I start; everywhere is my zero point.'

Emma was perturbed. 'You can see my death?'

'Yes, I can,' he smiled. 'Don't worry, Emma. It's a very long way away and you have a good and happy life. Things will get better for your mother, too. She has nothing to worry about. I won't tell you what's in store for you because that would spoil it. All I will say is that you'll love every minute of your life and you'll be happy and fulfilled. But what I will say is this: I'll be with you always and everywhere. You'll never lose me, Emma. And that makes me so happy. Merry Christmas, sweetheart.'

'Merry Christmas, Dad.'

'And thank you for thinking of your Mum. That photo looks pretty good in that new frame.'

That was what you got for watching silly old films when you were grieving, Emma told herself when she awoke. You got daft dreams about dead people and space and time, and crazy clocks with too many numbers. Yes, it was a nice dream, and even though it was a dream talking to her Dad had been comforting. But it wasn't real. He was still gone, still dead, and would never be back. For an instant the thought was too much to bear. But she forced the feeling away and the moment passed. She and her mother needed to be strong for each other.

It was nine in the morning. The heating was on and Emma could smell coffee, toast and eggs. She felt hungry for the first time since her father's accident. She visited the bathroom and went downstairs.

'Morning Mum – merry Christmas,' she announced.

'Merry Christmas, love. The coffee's ready but the eggs will be another minute.'

Emma drank half a mug of coffee while watching her mother scramble the eggs and spoon it onto slices of toast. She attacked her breakfast with unexpected relish. For once there was nothing left over for the birds and foxes. She felt a bit guilty about that and resolved to throw a few slices of bread out for them later.

When breakfast was finished they went into the lounge to open their presents. Emma felt guilty again, this time because all but one of the presents were for her. She opened the first one.

'Mum! A Kindle Fire! You shouldn't have, really. I mean, can you afford it?'

Her mother shrugged and smiled tiredly. 'We might as well spend it while we've got it, Em. Don't worry, love – none of the other stuff was anywhere near that expensive.'

Emma watched as her Mum unwrapped the picture frame. Her mother seemed surprised.

'Thanks, Em – the frame is absolutely lovely. This will be perfect for that photo I found when I was going through your father's things. It's just the right size.'

'What photo is that? Did you tell me about it?'

'To be honest, I can't remember. My head was all over the place at the time. It was on the digital camera I gave him last Christmas so it must have been taken recently. I can't think where, though. It's nowhere I know. Look, I printed it out.'

Emma's mother went to her bureau and retrieved a glossy five by eight inch colour print. 'Here you go, do you recognise it?'

The photograph had caught her father blowing a kiss at the camera, though that familiar smile was still very much in evidence. He was unshaven and needed a haircut. He was wearing jeans and a checked shirt, and he was barefoot. By his side was a large grandfather clock. The hands were touching the zero.

Mighty Boy

When I was a kid I knew a real superhero. He was my best friend. He was the same age as me, only a couple of days older. We lived in the same street, went to the same school and had the same friends. We liked the same films and television series and comics. He was the same height as me, skinny and dark-haired like me. We even looked alike. My mother used to joke that my father had been busy the year before we were born; my father made comments I didn't understand for a long time, about the milkman. Looking back, I realise he wasn't being humorous at all, but in those days I didn't know the stuff I know now. I was just a kid and the conflicts around me were too subtle to attract my attention and too complicated for me to understand when they did. For one thing, I didn't realise that my father was using the undoubted but entirely coincidental resemblance of his son to someone else's as a metaphorical stick to beat my mother with, the opening blows of a war that raged for years and ended, as all wars do, with too many losers.

But the similarities were outweighed by the differences. Because my friend was a superhero and I was not. His name was Edward but I called him Mighty Boy. I'd seen him in action and the name fitted him like a glove.

Mighty Boy could run really fast and for a long time. He ran everywhere. Although he was thin like me, he was much stronger than he looked. He could jump like a cat, swim like a fish and climb like a monkey; and when he had to fight he did it like a demon. Nobody ever beat him, not in anything. He also had the sharpest eyesight, most acute hearing and best sense of smell of anyone I ever met. Mighty Boy was very clever, good with his hands and quick-thinking.

I once saw Mighty Boy go over a brick wall that was higher than either of us. He simply ran toward it then seemed to walk up it at speed, resting one hand lightly on the top and vaulting effortlessly over it and into the garden on the other side. Sometimes he came into my garden like that. I'd watch him glide down across the lawn and onto our crazy-paving path, landing as softly and lightly as a butterfly alighting on a leaf. He could pass through impossibly narrow gaps without breaking his stride, negotiate tangled shrubbery and brambles without disturbing a single stem, and do it noiselessly enough that birds and sleeping hedgehogs weren't disturbed. I never knew him to break sweat or breathe hard.

Now, so many years later, I know that Mighty Boy was an early and unwitting exponent of the discipline called Parkour or 'free-running'. But where Parkour is a discipline that has to be learned and trained for, Mighty Boy simply had an instinctive awareness of his environment and his own capabilities, and was able to utilise those capabilities to the full within that environment. I realise now that I never saw him fail at anything because he never attempted anything he knew he couldn't do, whether he knew his limitations consciously or not. And there was one thing he would never be able to do, though that wouldn't matter for many years.

One afternoon after school, when we were nine, I found myself cornered by three of the bigger kids from a class two years above us. First they demanded money then, when I told them I didn't have any, started pushing me around. It got worse very quickly. One moment they were just shoving at me and hissing insults; then they began to hit me. I suffered that in near-silence for maybe a couple of minutes. But my passivity seemed only to inflame them and the biggest boy picked up a two-foot length of wood that was lying nearby.

Just as he raised the stick to beat me with it, a whirlwind materialised in our midst, a flailing fury of fists and feet that connected hard with everyone but me. Within seconds all three of my tormentors were on the ground, covering their heads and screaming for the newcomer to leave them alone. Two of them were crying, snivelling like slapped toddlers. And there he stood, absurdly magnificent in blue jeans and a yellow pullover, his face stern but calm. He held out a hand and helped me to my feet. In that bewildering melee I hadn't even noticed that I'd fallen down. As we walked away he started telling me about a new comic he'd got, for all the world as if nothing unusual had occurred.

Until then he'd been Edward – but at that moment it was clear to me that it was an inadequate and mundane name for such a fearsome, fearless creature. He'd never quite been ordinary but in my eyes that incident elevated him to the extraordinary, like Batman or Superman, the Flash or Green Lantern. From then on he was Mighty Boy, my hero – my superhero. I always pictured him patrolling the streets at night in his blue and yellow costume, masked and caped, fighting crime and foiling the world domination plans of megalomaniac arch-villains and their brutish henchmen. I saw him running up walls at breath-taking speed, dropping from trees and rooftops onto an assortment of crooks and evildoers, righteously beating them into submission – protecting the innocent, saving the world.

Those three bullies never bothered me again but there were others that tried. They always regretted it. Might Boy was my shield. I wrote little stories about him, fictionalising his real exploits and making up new ones, illustrated with pictures of Mighty Boy in the blue and yellow outfit he always wore in my imagination, drawn in black ballpoint and coloured with felts pins, the letters MB emblazoned on his chest in red. There he was, running, jumping, climbing and fighting the bad guys while I looked on, admiring his every move. As it was in real life, so it was in the stories I made up and the games I coerced him into playing. I was his Jimmy Olsen.

He went along with the games and stories but didn't like it when I called him a superhero. 'Proper superheroes can fly,' he would say in that unwaveringly reasonable tone. 'I can't fly, so I'm not a superhero, am I?' And the first time I called him Mighty Boy he became positively embarrassed. 'Nothing mighty about me, mate,' he said with a wry smile. 'Except that I'm mighty hungry. Got any sweets?'

He was always hungry, which doesn't surprise me now,

when I think of all the energy he must have used up in an average day; but back then I imagined him winning eating competitions. Mighty Boy ate a lot, and he ate very quickly. The food shovelled into his mouth was rapidly chewed, then swallowed as the next portion approached his lips. He ate like a machine. I doubt that he tasted much of what he consumed. But I suppose for him taste wasn't the point of food. It was fuel, nothing more. Though he was fond of those boiled sweets, the rhubarb and custard flavour. There would usually be one tucked away in his cheek while he was eating other stuff, ready to be popped back into place on his tongue when the fuel tank was full. Mighty Boy was always happy to mix business with pleasure.

Nothing much changed when we left primary school behind and started at the local comprehensive. The more aggressive of the boys who hadn't known us before soon learned to steer clear of Mighty Boy, and to leave me alone too. The teachers indulged us – Mighty Boy because he was so damned good at everything he turned his hand to, and me because I was his friend. One teacher used to call us the Conjoined Twins. When I found out what that meant I didn't know whether to feel insulted or flattered. In the end I opted for the latter because Might Boy was the coolest guy I knew and knowing that other people thought of us as a pair made me feel good.

Although my sexual preference has never been in question, I sometimes wonder if there was a homoerotic element to my adulation. But as far as I can see, most of the kids who have crushes on others of the some sex do so not because they want to go to bed with them but because they want to *be* them. I certainly didn't want to shag Mighty Boy.

The cheesy porn mags I kept hidden away from prying parents were exclusively of the naked woman variety. As far as I know, Mighty Boy's tastes were similar. Well, they would be, wouldn't they? We were practically identical twins, after all. But I'd be a liar if said he wasn't the only person in this world I ever truly admired, the one human being I looked up to – my very own superhero, the person I aspired to become. It may not have been sexual but I suppose it was a kind of romantic love. Isn't that what hero-worship is really about?

Secondary school was great, for both of us. Mighty Boy excelled at sports and games – he was in the school cricket and football teams, captain of the chess club, and ran in the district schools athletics championships. He was David Watts incarnate. I once saw him take six wickets in one over; and that followed an innings in which he scored a century off twenty balls. In the county schools cup final he scored a first-half hat-trick, went in goal when the regular keeper went off with an injury, and saved a penalty. He was indomitable, irresistible. It wasn't too long before his bedroom was adorned with cups and medals to complement the mandatory posters of rock stars and famous footballers. His academic success was as inevitable as the sun rising in the morning. He collected O and A levels like other kids collected stamps or cigarette cards. I didn't do too badly out of it – I was sort of dragged along in his wake. I couldn't really help doing fairly well.

We were finally separated when we left school. Neither of us fancied university so I went to work at the local branch of a well-known bank. Certain that Mighty Boy would sign up with one or other of the football or cricket clubs that were constantly knocking at his door, I was absolutely staggered when he took a job with a big landscape gardening firm. When I told him he was crazy, he just shrugged.

'Sport's meant to be fun,' he said. 'When you get paid for playing games, it stops being fun and becomes just another job. Even if I was good enough, that's not for me. Anyway, I like gardening and I love the idea of creating gardens for other people. I can still play football and cricket at weekends. Besides, with this job I'll get the chance to climb trees now and then, and you know how much I like climbing trees.'

There were other separations. My father's suspicions were voiced increasingly loudly and his behaviour tipped over into hostility and frequent, incoherent rages. Ironically, this drove my mother into the arms of a sympathetic and, I have to admit, much nicer man. Having watched helplessly and sometimes fearfully for years as she was systematically victimised, there was no way I could blame her – though I did resent her for leaving me with his self-righteous sullenness and occasional darker moods. Mighty Boy was supportive, but in a muted way.

'You know it's for the best,' he said.

'Yeah,' I agreed. 'But it's still pretty hard to take. Dad's impossible to live with now she's gone. Mum told me she'd never been unfaithful to him until he started threatening to hit her. She said as far as she was concerned their marriage ended that day and she reckoned she was free to look for someone else if she wanted to. Dad just sees it as vindication. It's his own bloody fault but he still blames her. You know, he's actually talking about making me take a

DNA test. I think he really does believe that me and you have the same father.'

'Well, it won't be my old man,' said Mighty Boy. 'I don't think he's got the gumption to have a bit on the side.'

'Maybe it was the milkman after all,' I suggested with a grin.

Mighty Boy shook his head. 'I shouldn't think so. I don't think my mum has the gumption for playing around, either.'

And so we grew up. I settled in at the bank, cheerfully resigned to an existence of exchanging hours of boredom for a good salary and perks, and left home as soon as I could find an affordable flat. After a few years I was promoted, promoted again, and found myself a steady girlfriend I supposed I would eventually marry.

But first my dad remarried and began a new cycle of jealousy and suspicion, though he still bitched about my mother at every opportunity. His new woman was a likeable sort and I got on well with her. She wasn't as patient as my mother, though. She lasted eighteen months before voting with her feet. One day she simply wasn't there anymore. My father was the only person who didn't see it coming. It gave him someone else to complain about but I never listened. I'd heard it all before; and besides, I have no sympathy for self-inflicted damage.

Mighty Boy – he nagged me to drop the nickname so he was now Edward again – did pretty well for himself, too. His creativity blossomed and he began to get a reputation as a garden designer. He contributed articles to gardening magazines and racked up a few appearances on Radio 4's *Gardener's Question Time*. One day, when we were thirty, over a few beers he confided that he was being courted by two rival television companies to appear in new garden makeover programmes. He was excited by these developments and I was pleased for him. For all that I'd done well in life, he was still my hero and I wanted him to do better than me. Because that was how it was meant to be.

I waited for the news to break but it never did. I waited for Edward to call me but he didn't. My own calls and e-mails went unanswered. I knocked on his door but there were no lights and the door remained unopened. Then, through third parties, I heard my friend had gone abroad for an extended holiday – France or Spain, Brazil or Thailand. It changed from one source to the next. Someone else said he'd emigrated, though they weren't sure if it was to Australia or the USA. Another person thought he'd been killed in a skiing accident – or was it paragliding? I was perplexed. Surely Edward wouldn't have gone away without telling me? I was his closest friend, for God's sake. Even if he'd been hurt or had died, his parents still lived in the same street as my father, and neighbours talk.

The days stretched into weeks. Before I knew it, several months had passed without so much as a single word from him. Of course, I had work and romance to take my mind off Edward's fate. But it wasn't enough. I worried more with every day that passed without him contacting me. Even the gossip had dried up. Nobody spoke about him anymore. I called on his mother but she was as upset and worried as I was. His flat remained dark and silent. Mighty Boy had seemingly vanished.

Then, out of the blue, he phoned. Late one night, after

nearly six months of silence, he called. He sounded the same as he always had. At first there was nothing in his voice or the words he spoke to make me suspect that anything was wrong. Nothing could be wrong, could it? He was Edward, formerly the superhero Mighty Boy, and he'd just been away on some mysterious errand. Perhaps, I thought whimsically, he'd been constructing an underground bunker or Fortress of Solitude in the Antarctic or somewhere on the Siberian tundra. Maybe he'd been on a secret mission to save the world from sinister arch-villains and their evil henchmen. What the hell, to me he was still Mighty Boy and I believed he could do just about anything he wanted. But he was hopeless at one of the most important things there is.

He was crap at relationships. Despite never being short of admirers, Edward had never coaxed a girlfriend past three months of involvement, had parted acrimoniously from most of them, and had proved a major disappointment to any woman that had ever gone out with him. It wasn't that he treated them badly – just that he couldn't communicate with them. Seeing him in the company of women was as distressing to me as it clearly was for him. He was awkward, tongue-tied and helpless in their presence. Sporting prowess and academic achievement were no help at all in the crucial matter of dealing with the opposite sex. He was utterly hopeless at it, and I couldn't see any way that it was ever going to get better. So I continued to imagine him as the solitary hero of my boyhood fantasies. I was too afraid for him to face up to the alternative, the likelihood that he would grow old alone and unloved.

'Where are you?' I asked when the preliminary chat was concluded.

'Beachy Head,' he replied, as calm as you like. 'It's a lovely evening. Thought I'd go for a good, long cross-country run. I think it might rain later, though.'

My stomach lurched. Everyone knows why people go to Beachy Head. The bottom of that precipice is littered with grief. I tried to sound unconcerned. 'What are you doing there?'

'I'm looking at the sea and the stars. I can see a ship out there, a ferry or something.'

'Well, just stay away from the edge, OK?'

He laughed quietly. 'I'm right at the edge now, mate. Actually, I've been at the edge for a long time. I just didn't know it.'

'For Christ's sake, Edward – stop fucking about and just come home, eh?'

'Did you ever guess how much I envy you?'

'What – you envy *me*? Are you serious?'

'I'm deadly serious. You're good at the one thing I could never do even a little bit well. You know how to do love, and I don't. I feel so bloody lonely all the time.'

I didn't know how to respond to that. 'Edward, don't be so bloody silly,' was all I could think to say.

'I'm not being silly – I'm being honest. Do you know what love is? It's all sparks and ashes, mate. Love begins with a spark. The spark makes a flame and you have to work to keep it alight, feed it and nurture it and protect it. If you don't, the fire dies down and all you're left with is ash. I can't keep the flames alight. I either don't try hard enough or I just can't do it – I don't even know which it is. All I have are little piles of ash, all that's left of the flames I couldn't keep going. I know I'll never have anything else. You, though – you have a flame and I know you'll do what it takes to make sure it never goes out.'

'Edward, you're not making sense.'

'It makes perfect sense to me. Look at your mum and dad. When we were little they were a great couple, but then your old man started getting all jealous and possessive, turned into a real control freak. Your mum couldn't handle it, took off with that bloke, and that was that. Your dad suffocated his flame. My folks – well, theirs just sort of died down to nothing. I'm not sure there was ever much of a spark to begin with. Affection wasn't exactly plentiful in my home. Now they're like two strangers forced to live in the same house. At least they're polite about it. I suppose that's something.'

'You're not your parents, Edward. I'm not mine. We don't have to be like them. I won't make the same mistakes my father made.'

'Maybe you won't, but I will. Maybe my trouble is that I don't know how to strike the balance between letting the flame breathe and keeping it close. Maybe I just don't understand women. I mess up every time. Little piles of ash.'

'You'll get it right one day,' I told him. 'You'll do it when it matters.'

'It always matters to me. Nothing else ever really did. You remember all those games we used to play, all those special things I imagined I'd do one day? Scoring hat-tricks, saving penalties, knocking sixes, taking wickets?'

No, I didn't remember those games. What I

remembered were the cheering crowds, the victories and the plaudits. Or did I? 'But you were so good at sport. You had trophies, there were talent scouts. You were the best player in the chess club. You were good academically, too. Look at all those exam passes.'

'You made them up,' he said, so simply and brutally that it was like being punched hard in the gut. 'You made all of it up.'

For a few seconds I refused to believe what I'd just heard. 'I don't understand,' I said. 'What do you mean?'

'You always used to talk about me playing for the Blues or the county cricket club, as if it was something that was bound to happen. And yeah, I passed the exams, but only just. My grades weren't crap but they weren't great. I was good at a lot of things but I was never *that* good. All I was ever really exceptional at was climbing and jumping and running around all over the place. You believed your own dreams and you ignored mine. You remember when I took short-cuts through people's gardens? That was because I really liked gardens and wanted to look at them. I always wanted to be a gardener.'

'Well then,' I said, forcing a smile, hoping it would be transmitted through my voice. 'At least you've done that.'

'Yeah,' he replied quietly. 'But I don't have anyone to do it for.'

There was an uncomfortable pause. I have no idea what was going through his mind but I was silent because the cherished beliefs of my youth were burning around me, crumbling to ashes. That's how childhood imagination can seduce you, how the stories and myths you weave in and about the past can give false comfort. I was a grown man, an adult with responsibilities, and I knew full well that Mighty Boy was really only Edward – a talented and reasonably accomplished man, but still only a man and as fallible and flawed as any other. He had been, I suppose, my ideal of what a human being could and should be. Deep down, I knew I'd spent most of my life exaggerating his abilities and accomplishments because it gave me hope for my own perfectibility. Those amazing sporting feats? I swear I witnessed them; but I knew they were not in the school records. The football team didn't even reach the cup final that year. Teachers I bumped into in the street in the years after I left school recalled him with affection but not admiration. That was when I should have begun to understand that because he was good at so many things I'd accepted his excellence at everything. That was when I should have realised that my hero was my own creation, that like all worshippers – like all lovers – I'd placed the object of my adoration on a pedestal far too lofty for him.

'Hey,' he said at last. 'Call me "Mighty Boy" again, like you used to.'

I grinned in spite of my sudden emptiness and growing unease. 'OK, I will – Mighty Boy.'

'That's good,' he said with a sad laugh. 'Because I think maybe I'm a superhero after all.'

'What do mean?'

'I think I can fly now,' he said.

Then all I could hear was the crackle and rush of air against the microphone as he took to the sky.

About the Author

Alby Stone was born and raised in Southend-on-Sea in Essex and now lives and works in London. He has written several non-fiction books, a number of articles, and a few novels and short stories.

http://vaingloriouslunacy.com
http://clerkenwellwritersasylum.wordpress.com/

Printed in Great Britain
by Amazon